D1029815

CAT O' NINE TALES

And Other Stories

Also by Jeffrey Archer

NOVELS

Not a Penny More, Not a Penny Less
Shall We Tell the President?
Kane & Abel
The Prodigal Daughter
First Among Equals
A Matter of Honor
As the Crow Flies
Honor Among Thieves
The Fourth Estate
The Eleventh Commandment
Sons of Fortune
False Impression

SHORT STORIES

A Quiver Full of Arrows
A Twist in the Tale
Twelve Red Herrings
To Cut a Long Story Short
The Collected Short Stories

PLAYS

Beyond Reasonable Doubt
Exclusive
The Accused

PRISON DIARIES

Volume One – Hell
Volume Two – Purgatory
Volume Three – Heaven

SCREENPLAYS

Mallory: Walking off the Map
False Impression

JEFFREY ARCHER

CAT O' NINE TALES

And Other Stories

WITHDRAWN

Drawings by Ronald Searle

**Doubleday Large Print
Home Library Edition**

St. Martin's Press ❧ New York

CAT O' NINE TALES. Copyright © 2007 by Jeffrey Archer. All rights reserved. Printed in the United States of America. No part of this book may be used or reproduced in any manner whatsoever without written permission except in the case of brief quotations embodied in critical articles or reviews. For information, address St. Martin's Press, 175 Fifth Avenue, New York, N.Y. 10010.

Drawings copyright © 2007 by Ronald Searle

ISBN-13: 978-0-7394-8462-3

First published in Great Britian by Macmillan, an imprint of Pan Macmillan Ltd.

First U.S. Edition: June 2007

**This Large Print Book carries the
Seal of Approval of N.A.V.H.**

For Elizabeth

Contents

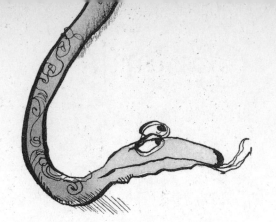

Preface

While I was incarcerated for two years, in five different prisons, I picked up several stories that were not appropriate to include in the day-to-day journals of a prison diary. These tales are marked in the contents with an asterisk.

Although all nine stories have been embellished, each is rooted in fact. In all but one, the prisoner concerned has asked me not to reveal his real name.

The other three stories included in this volume are also true, but I came across them after being released from prison: in Athens – 'A Greek Tragedy', in London – 'The Wisdom of Solomon', and in Rome my favourite – 'In the Eye of the Beholder'.

The Man Who Robbed His Own Post Office

The Beginning

Mr. Justice Gray stared down at the two defendants in the dock. Chris and Sue Haskins had pleaded guilty to the theft of £250,000, being the property of the Post Office, and to falsifying four passports.

Mr. and Mrs. Haskins looked about the same age, which was hardly surprising as they had been at school together some forty years before. You could have passed them in the street without giving either of them a second look. Chris was about five foot nine, his dark wavy hair turning gray, and he was at least a stone overweight. He stood upright in the dock, and although his suit was well worn, his shirt was clean and his striped tie suggested that he was a member of a club. His black shoes looked as if they had been spit-and-polished every morning. His wife Sue stood by his side. Her neat floral dress and sensible shoes hinted at an organized and tidy woman, but then they were both wearing the clothes that they would normally have worn to church. After all, they considered the law to be nothing less than an extension of the Almighty.

Mr. Justice Gray turned his attention to Mr. and Mrs. Haskins's barrister, a young man who had been selected on the grounds of cost, rather than experience.

"No doubt you wish to suggest there are mitigating circumstances in this case, Mr. Rodgers," prompted the judge helpfully.

"Yes, m'lord," admitted the newly qualified barrister as he rose from his place. He would like to have told his lordship that this was only his second case, but he felt his lordship would be unlikely to consider that a mitigating circumstance.

Mr. Justice Gray settled back as he prepared to listen to how poor Mr. Haskins had been thrashed by a ruthless stepfather, night after night, and Mrs. Haskins had been raped by an evil uncle at an impressionable age, but no; Mr. Rodgers assured the court that the Haskins came from happy, well-balanced backgrounds and had in fact been at school together. Their only child, Tracey, a graduate of Bristol University, was now working as an estate agent in Ashford. A model family.

Mr. Rodgers glanced down at his brief before going on to explain how the Haskins had ended up in the dock that morning. Mr. Justice Gray became more and more intrigued by their tale, and by the time the barrister had resumed his place the judge felt he needed a little more time to consider the length of the sentence. He ordered the two defendants to appear before him the following Monday at ten o'clock in the forenoon, by which time he would have come to a decision.

Mr. Rodgers rose a second time.

"You were no doubt hoping that I would grant your clients bail, Mr. Rodgers?" inquired the judge, raising an eyebrow, and before the surprised young barrister could respond Mr. Justice Gray said, "Granted."

* * *

Jasper Gray told his wife about the plight of Mr. and Mrs. Haskins over lunch on Sunday. Long before the judge had devoured his rack of lamb, Vanessa Gray had offered her opinion.

"Sentence them both to an hour of community service, and then issue a court order instructing the Post Office to return their original investment in full," she declared, revealing a common sense not always bestowed on the male of the species. To do him justice, the judge agreed with his spouse, although he told her that he would never get away with it.

"Why not?" she asked.

"Because of the four passports."

Mr. Justice Gray was not surprised to find Mr. and Mrs. Haskins standing dutifully in the dock at ten o'clock the following morning. After all, they were not criminals.

The judge raised his head, stared down at them and tried to look grave. "You have both pleaded guilty to the crimes of theft from a post office and of falsifying four passports." He didn't bother to add any adjectives such as evil, heinous or even dis-

graceful, as he didn't consider them appropriate on this occasion. "You have therefore left me with no choice," he continued, "but to send you both to prison." The judge turned his attention to Chris Haskins. "You were obviously the instigator of this crime, and with that in mind, I sentence you to three years' imprisonment." Chris Haskins was unable to hide his surprise: his barrister had warned him to expect at least five years. Chris had to stop himself from saying, thank you, my lord.

The judge then looked across at Mrs. Haskins. "I accept that your part in this conspiracy was possibly no more than an act of loyalty to your husband. However, you are well aware of the difference between right and wrong, and therefore I shall send you to prison for one year."

"My lord," protested Chris Haskins.

Mr. Justice Gray frowned for the first time. He was not in the habit of being interrupted while passing sentence. "Mr. Haskins, if it is your intention to appeal against my judgment—"

"Certainly not, my lord," said Chris Haskins, interrupting the judge for a second time. "I was just wondering if you would allow me to serve my wife's sentence."

Mr. Justice Gray was so taken aback by the request that he couldn't think of a suitable reply to a question he had never been asked before. He banged his hammer, stood up and quickly left the courtroom. An usher hurriedly shouted, "All rise."

Chris and Sue first met in the playground of their local primary school in Cleethorpes, a seaside town on the east coast of England. Chris was standing in a queue waiting for his third of a pint of milk—government regulation for all schoolchildren under the age of sixteen. Sue was the milk monitor. Her job was to make sure everyone received their correct allocation. As she handed over the little bottle to Chris, neither of them gave the other a second look. Sue was in the class above Chris, so they rarely came across each other during the day, except when Chris was standing in the milk queue. At the end of the year Sue passed her eleven-plus and took up a place at the local grammar school. Chris was appointed the new milk monitor. The following September he also passed his eleven-plus, and joined Sue at Cleethorpes Grammar.

They remained oblivious to each other throughout their school days until Sue became head girl. After that, Chris couldn't help but notice her because at the end of morning assembly she would read out the school notices for the day. Bossy was the adjective most often trotted out by the lads whenever Sue's name came up in conversation (strange how women in positions of authority so often acquire the sobriquet *bossy*, while a man holding the same rank is somehow invested with qualities of leadership).

When Sue left at the end of the year Chris once again forgot all about her. He did not follow in her illustrious footsteps and become head boy, although he had a successful—by his standards—if somewhat uneventful year. He played for the school's second eleven cricket team, came fifth in the cross-country match against Grimsby Grammar, and did well enough in his final exams for them to be unworthy of mention either way.

No sooner had Chris left school than he received a letter from the Ministry of Defense, instructing him to report to his local recruiting office to sign up for a spell of National Service—a two-year compulsory period for all boys at the age of eighteen, when they had to serve in the armed forces. Chris's only choice in the matter was between the Army, the Royal Navy or the Royal Air Force.

He selected the RAF, and even spent a fleeting moment wondering what it might be like to be a jet pilot. Once Chris had passed his medical and filled in all the necessary forms at the local recruiting office, the duty sergeant handed him a rail pass to somewhere called Mablethorpe; he was to report to the guardhouse by eight o'clock on the first of the month.

Chris spent the next twelve weeks being put through basic training, along with a hundred and twenty other raw recruits. He quickly discovered that only one applicant in a thousand was selected to be a pilot. Chris was not one in a thousand. At the end of the twelve weeks he was given the choice of working in the canteen, the officers' mess, the quartermaster's stores or flight operations. He opted for flight operations, and was allocated a job in the stores.

It was when he reported for duty the following Monday that he once again met up with Sue, or to be more accurate Corporal Sue Smart. She was inevitably standing at the head of the line; this time giving out job instructions. Chris didn't immediately recognize her, dressed in her smart blue uniform with her hair almost hidden under a cap. In any case, he was admiring her shapely legs when she said, "Haskins, report to the quartermaster's stores." Chris raised his head. It was that voice he could never forget.

"Sue?" he ventured tentatively. Corporal Smart looked up from her clipboard and glared at the recruit who dared to address her by her first name. She recognized the face, but couldn't place him.

"Chris Haskins," he volunteered.

"Ah, yes, Haskins," she said, and hesitated before adding, "report to Sergeant Travis in the stores, and he'll brief you on your duties."

"Yes, Corp," Chris replied and quickly disappeared off in the direction of the quartermaster's stores. As he walked away, Chris didn't notice that Sue was taking a second look.

Chris didn't come across Corporal Smart again until his first weekend leave. He spotted her sitting at the other end of a railway carriage on the journey back to Cleethorpes. He made no attempt to join her, even pretending not to see her. However, he did find himself looking up from time to time, admiring her slim figure—he didn't remember her being as pretty as that.

When the train pulled into Cleethorpes station, Chris spotted his mother chatting to another woman. He knew immediately who she must be—the same red hair, the same trim figure, the same . . .

"Hello, Chris," Mrs. Smart greeted him as

he joined his mother on the platform. "Was Sue on the train with you?"

"I didn't notice," said Chris, as Sue walked up to join them.

"I expect you see a lot of each other now you're based at the same camp," suggested Chris's mother.

"No, not really," said Sue, trying to sound disinterested.

"Well, we'd better be off," said Mrs. Haskins. "I have to give Chris and his dad dinner before they go off to watch the football," she explained.

"Do you remember him?" asked Mrs. Smart as Chris and his mother walked along the platform toward the exit.

"Snotty Haskins?" Sue hesitated. "Can't say I do."

"Oh, you like him that much, do you?" said Sue's mother with a smile.

When Chris boarded the train that Sunday evening, Sue was already sitting in her place at the end of the carriage. Chris was about to walk straight past her and find a seat in the next carriage, when he heard her say, "Hi, Chris, did you have a nice weekend?"

"Not bad, Corp," said Chris, stopping to look down at her. "Grimsby beat Lincoln three–one, and I'd forgotten how good the fish and chips are in Cleethorpes compared to camp."

Sue smiled. "Why don't you join me?" she said, patting the seat beside her. "And I think it will be all right to call me Sue when we're not in barracks."

On the journey back to Mablethorpe, Sue did most of the talking, partly because Chris was so smitten with her—could this be the same skinny little girl who had handed out the milk each morning?—and partly because he realized the bubble would burst the moment they set foot back in camp. Non-commissioned officers just don't fraternize with the ranks.

The two of them parted at the camp gates and went their separate ways. Chris walked back to the barracks, while Sue headed off for the NCO quarters. When Chris strolled into his Nissen hut to join his fellow conscripts, one of them was bragging about the WRAF he'd had it off with. He even went into graphic detail, describing what RAF knickers look like. "A dark shade of blue held up by thick elastic," he assured the mesmerized onlookers. Chris lay on his bed and stopped listening to the unlikely tale, as his thoughts returned to Sue. He wondered how long it would be before he saw her again.

Not as long as he feared because when Chris went to the canteen for lunch the following day he spotted Sue sitting in the corner with a group of girls from the ops room. He wanted to stroll across to her table and, like David Niven, casually ask her out on a date. There was a Doris Day film showing at the Odeon that he thought she might enjoy, but he'd sooner have walked across a minefield than interrupt her while his mates were watching.

Chris selected his lunch from the counter—a bowl of vegetable soup, sausage and chips, and custard pie. He carried his tray across to a table on the other side of the room and joined a group of his fellow conscripts. He was tucking into the custard pie, while discussing Grimsby's chances against Blackpool, when he felt a hand touch his shoulder. He looked round to see Sue smiling down at him. Everyone else at the table stopped talking. Chris turned a bright shade of red.

"Doing anything on Saturday night?" Sue asked. The red deepened to crimson as he shook his head. "I was thinking of going to see *Calamity Jane*." She paused. "Care to join me?" Chris nodded. "Why don't we meet outside the camp gates at six?" Another nod. Sue smiled. "See you then." Chris turned back to find his friends staring at him in awe.

Chris didn't remember much about the film because he spent most of his time trying to summon up enough courage to put his arm round Sue's shoulder. He didn't even manage it when Howard Keel kissed Doris Day. However, after they left the cinema and walked back toward the waiting bus, Sue took his hand.

"What are you going to do once you've finished your National Service?" Sue asked as the last bus took them back to camp.

"Join my dad on the buses, I suppose," said Chris. "How about you?"

"Once I've served three years, I have to decide if I want to become an officer, and make the RAF my career."

"I hope you come back and work in Cleethorpes," Chris blurted out.

* * *

Chris and Sue Haskins were married a year later in St. Aidan's parish church.

After the wedding, the bride and groom set off for Newhaven in a hired car, intending to spend their honeymoon on the south coast of Portugal. After only a few days on the Algarve, they ran out of money. Chris drove them back to Cleethorpes, but vowed that they would return to Albufeira just as soon as he could afford it.

Chris and Sue began married life by renting three rooms on the ground floor of a semi-detached in Jubilee Road. The two milk monitors were unable to hide their contentment from anyone who came into contact with them.

Chris joined his father on the buses and became a conductor with the Green Line Municipal Coach Company, while Sue was employed as a trainee with a local insurance company. A year later Sue gave birth to Tracey and left her job to bring up their daughter. This spurred Chris on to work even harder and seek promotion. With the occasional prod from Sue, Chris began to study for the company's promotion exam. Four years later Chris was appointed an inspector. All boded well in the Haskins household.

When Tracey informed her father that she wanted a pony for Christmas, he had to point out that they didn't have a garden. Chris compromised, and on Tracey's seventh birthday presented her with a Labrador puppy, which they christened Corp. The Haskins family wanted for nothing, and that might have been the end of this tale if Chris hadn't got the sack. It happened thus.

The Green Line Municipal Coach Company was taken over by the Hull Carriage Bus Company. With the merger of the two firms, job losses became inevitable, and Chris was among those offereda redundancy package. The only alternative the new management came up with was the reinstatement of Chris as a conductor. Chris turned his nose up at the offer. He felt confi-

dent of finding another job, and therefore accepted the settlement.

It wasn't long before the redundancy money ran out, and despite Ted Heath's promise of a brave new world, Chris quickly discovered that alternative employment wasn't that easy to find in Cleethorpes. Sue never once complained and, now that Tracey was going to school, took on a part-time job at Parsons, a local fish-and-chip shop. Not only did this bring in a weekly wage, supplemented by the occasional tip, but it also allowed Chris to enjoy a large plate of cod and chips every lunchtime.

Chris continued to try and find a job. He visited the employment exchange every morning, except on Friday, when he stood in a long line, waiting to collect his meager unemployment benefit. After twelve months of failed interviews, and sorry-you-don't-seem-to-have-the-necessary-qualifications, Chris became anxious enough to seriously consider returning to his old job as a bus conductor. Sue assured him that it wouldn't be long before he was once again promoted to inspector.

Meanwhile, Sue took on more responsibility at the fish-and-chip shop and a year later was made assistant manager. Once again, this tale might have reached its natural conclusion, except this time it was Sue who was given her notice.

She warned Chris over a fish supper that Mr. and Mrs. Parsons were considering early retirement and planning to put the shop up for sale.

"How much are they expecting it to fetch?"

"I heard Mr. Parsons mention the figure of five thousand pounds."

"Then let's hope the new owners know a good thing when they see it," said Chris, forking another chip.

"The new owners are far more likely to come with their own staff. Don't forget what happened to you when the bus company was taken over."

Chris thought about it.

At eight thirty the following morning, Sue left the house to take Tracey to school, before going on to work. Once the two of them had departed, Chris and Corp set out for their morning constitutional. The dog was puzzled when his master didn't head for the beach, where he could enjoy his usual frolic in the waves, but instead marched off in the opposite direction, toward the center of the town. Corp loyally bounded after him, and ended up being tied to a railing outside the Midland Bank in the High Street.

The manager of the bank could not hide his surprise when Mr. Haskins requested an interview to discuss a business venture. He quickly checked Mr. and Mrs. Haskins' joint bank account, to find that they were seventeen pounds and twelve shillings in credit. He was pleased to note that they had never run up an overdraft, despite Mr. Haskins being out of work for over a year.

The manager listened sympathetically to his client's proposal, but sadly shook his head even before Chris had come to the end of his well-rehearsed presentation.

"The bank couldn't consider such a risk," the manager explained, "at least not while you have so little security to offer as collateral. You don't even own your own home," the banker pointed out. Chris thanked him, shook him by the hand and left undaunted.

He crossed the High Street, tied Corp to another railing and entered Martins Bank. Chris had to wait for quite some time before the manager was able to see him. He was greeted with the same response, but at least on this occasion the manager recommended that Chris should approach Britannia Finance, who, he explained, were a new company specializing in start-up loans for small businesses. Chris thanked him, left the bank, untied Corp and jogged back to Jubilee Road, arriving only moments before Sue returned home with his lunch: cod and chips.

After lunch, Chris left the house and headed for the nearest phone box. He put four pennies in the box and pressed button A. The conversation lasted for less than a minute. He then returned home, but didn't tell Sue who he had an appointment with the following day.

The next day Chris waited for Sue to take Tracey off to school before he slipped back upstairs to their bedroom. He took off his jeans and sweater, and replaced them with the suit he'd worn at his wedding, a cream shirt he only put on for church on Sundays, and a tie his mother-in-law had given him for Christmas, which he thought he'd never wear. He then shone his shoes until even his old drill sergeant would have agreed that they passed muster. He checked himself in the mirror, hoping he looked like the potential manager of a new business venture. He left the dog in the back garden, and headed into town.

Chris was fifteen minutes early for his meeting with a Mr. Tremaine, the loans manager with Britannia Finance Company. He was asked to take a seat in the waiting room. Chris picked up a copy of the *Financial Times* for the first time in his life. He couldn't find the sports pages. Fifteen minutes later a secretary ushered him through to Mr. Tremaine's office.

The loans executive listened with sympathy to Chris's ambitious proposal, and then inquired, just as the two bank managers had, "What security do you have to offer?"

"Nothing," replied Chris without guile, "other than the fact that my wife and I will work all the hours we're awake, and she already knows the business backward." Chris waited to hear the many reasons why Britannia couldn't consider his request.

Instead Mr. Tremaine asked, "As your wife would constitute half of our investment, what does she think about this whole enterprise?"

"I haven't even discussed it with her yet," Chris blurted out.

"Then I suggest you do so," said Mr. Tremaine, "and fairly quickly, because before we would consider investing in Mr. and Mrs. Haskins, we will need to meet Mrs. Haskins in order to find out if she's half as good as you claim."

Chris broke the news to his wife over supper that evening. Sue was speechless. A problem Chris had not come up against all that often in the past.

Once Mr. Tremaine had met Mrs. Haskins, it was only a matter of filling in countless forms before Britannia Finance advanced them a loan of £5,000. A month later Mr. and Mrs. Haskins moved from their three rooms in Jubilee Road to a fish-and-chip shop on Beach Street.

The Middle

Chris and Sue spent their first Sunday scraping the name *PARSONS* off the front of the shop, and painting in *HASKINS: under new management*. Sue quickly set about teaching Chris how to prepare the right ingredients to make the finest batter. If it was that easy, she kept reminding him, there wouldn't be a queue outside one chippy while a rival a few yards up the road remained empty. It was some weeks before Chris could guarantee his chips were always crisp and not hard or, worse, soggy. While he became the front-of-house manager, wrapping up the fish and dispensing the salt and vinegar, Sue took her place behind the till and collected the takings. In the evening, Sue always brought the books up to date, but she didn't go upstairs to join Chris in their little self-contained flat until the shop was spotless and you could see your face in the counter-top.

Sue was always the last to finish, but then Chris was the first to rise in the morning. He would be up by four o'clock, pull on an old tracksuit and head off for the docks with Corp. He returned a couple of hours later, having selected the finest cod, hake, skate and plaice, moments after the trawlers had docked with their morning catch.

Although Cleethorpes has several fish-and-chip shops, it was not long before a queue began to form outside Haskins, sometimes even before Sue had turned the closed sign round to allow the first customer to enter the shop. The queue never slackened between the hours of eleven a.m. and three p.m., or from five to nine in the evening, when the sign would finally be turned back round—but not until the last customer had been served.

At the end of their first year the Haskins declared a profit of just over £900. As the queues lengthened, the debt to Britannia Finance diminished, so they were able to return the loan in full, with interest, eight months before the five-year agreement ended.

During the next decade, the Haskins' reputation grew on land, as well as sea, which resulted in Chris being invited to join the Cleethorpes Rotary Club, and Sue becoming deputy chairman of the Mothers' Union.

On their twentieth wedding anniversary Sue and Chris returned to Portugal for a second honeymoon. They stayed in a four-star hotel for a fortnight and this time they didn't have to come home early. Mr. and Mrs. Haskins returned to Albufeira every summer for the next ten years. Creatures of habit, the Haskins.

Tracey left Cleethorpes Grammar School to attend Bristol University, where she studied business management. The only sadness in the Haskins' life was when Corp died. But then he was fourteen years old.

Chris was enjoying a drink with some fellow Rotarians when Dave Quenton, the manager of the town's most prestigious post office, told him that he was moving to the

Lake District and planning to sell his interest in the business.

This time Chris did discuss his latest proposal with his wife. Sue was once again taken by surprise and, when she recovered, needed several questions answered before she agreed to pay a return visit to Britannia Finance.

"How much do you have on deposit with the Midland Bank?" asked Mr. Tremaine, recently promoted to loans manager.

Sue checked her ledger. "Thirty-seven thousand, four hundred and eight pounds," she replied.

"And what value have you put on the fish-and-chip shop?" was his next question.

"We will be considering offers over one hundred thousand," said Sue confidently.

"And how much has the post office been valued at, remembering that it's in such a prime location?"

"Mr. Quenton says that the Post Office is looking for two hundred and seventy thousand, but he assures me they would settle for a quarter of a million, if they can find a suitable applicant."

"So you're likely to be a little over one hundred thousand short of your target," said the analyst, not having to refer to a ledger. He paused. "What was the post office's turnover last year?"

"Two hundred and thirty thousand pounds," replied Sue.

"Profit?"

Once again, Sue needed to check her figures. "Twenty-six thousand, four hundred, but that doesn't include the added bonus of spacious living accommodation, with rates and taxes covered in the annual return." She paused. "And this time we would own the property."

"If all those figures can be confirmed by our accountants," said Mr. Tremaine, "and you are able to sell the fish-and-chip shop for around a hundred thousand, it certainly appears to be a sound investment. But . . ." The two would-be clients looked apprehensive. "And there always is a but, when it comes to lending money. The loan would, of course, be subject to the post office maintaining its category A status. Property in that area is currently trading at around twenty thousand, so the real value of the post office is as a business, and only then if, I repeat, if, it continues to have category A status."

"But it's been a category A post office for the past thirty years," said Chris. "Why should that change in the future?"

"If I could predict the future, Mr. Haskins," replied the analyst, "I would never make a bad investment, but as I can't I have to take the occasional risk. Britannia invests in people, and on that front you have nothing to prove." He smiled. "We would, as with our first investment, expect any loan to be repaid in quarterly instalments, over a period of five years, and on this occasion, as such a large sum is involved, we would want to take a charge over the property."

"At what percentage?" demanded Chris.

"Eight and a half percent, with added penalties should increments not be paid on time."

"We'll need to consider your offer carefully," said Sue, "and we'll let you know once we've made our decision."

Mr. Tremaine stifled a smile.

"What was all that about category A status?" asked Sue as they walked quickly back toward the seafront, still hoping to open the shop in time for their first customer.

"Category A is where all the profits are," said Chris. "Savings accounts, pensions, postal orders, vehicle road tax and even premium bonds all guarantee you a handsome profit. Without them, you have to rely on TV licenses, stamps, electricity bills, and perhaps a little extra income if they allow you to run a shop on the side. If that was all Mr. Quenton had to offer, we'd be better off continuing to run the fish-and-chip shop."

"And is there any risk of us losing our category A status?" asked Sue.

"None whatsoever," said Chris, "or that's what the area manager assured me, and he's a fellow member of Rotary. He told me that the matter has never even come up for discussion at headquarters, and you can be pretty confident that Britannia will also have checked that out long before they would be willing to part with a hundred thousand."

"So you still think we should go ahead?"

"With a few refinements to their terms," said Chris.

"Like what?"

"Well, to start with, I've no doubt that Mr. Tremaine will come down to eight percent, now that the High Street banks have also begun investing in business ventures, and don't forget, this time he will have a charge over the property."

The Haskins sold their fish-and-chip shop for £112,000 and were able to add a further £38,000 from their credit account. Britannia topped it up with a loan of £100,000 at 8 percent. A check for £250,000 was sent to Post Office headquarters in London.

"Time to celebrate," declared Chris.

"What do you have in mind?" asked Sue. "Because we can't afford to spend any more money."

"Let's drive down to Ashford and spend the weekend with our daughter—" he paused—"and on the way back . . ."

"And on the way back?" repeated Sue.

"Let's drop into Battersea Dogs' Home."

A month later, Mr. and Mrs. Haskins and Stamps, another Labrador, this time black, moved from their fish-and-chip shop on Beach Street to a category A post office in Victoria Crescent.

Chris and Sue quickly returned to working hours that they hadn't experienced since they first opened the fish-and-chip shop. For the next five years they cut down on any little extras, and even went without holidays, although they often thought about another trip to Portugal, but that had to be put on hold until they completed their quarterly payments to Britannia. Chris continued to carry out his Rotary Club duties, while Sue became chairman of the Cleethorpes branch of the Mothers' Union. Tracey was promoted to sites manager, and Stamps ate more food than the three of them put together.

In their fourth year, Mr. and Mrs. Haskins won the "Area Post Office of the Year" award, and nine months later paid off the final instalment to Britannia.

The board of Britannia invited Chris and Sue to join them for lunch at the Royal Hotel to celebrate the fact that they now owned the post office without a penny of debt to their name.

"We still have to earn back our original investment," Chris reminded them. "A mere matter of two hundred and fifty thousand pounds."

"If you keep going at your present rate," suggested the chairman of Britannia, "it should only take you another five years to achieve and then you could be sitting on a business worth over a million."

"Does that mean I'm a millionaire?" asked Chris.

"No, it does not," butted in Sue. "Our current account is showing a credit of a little over ten thousand pounds. You're a ten thousandaire."

The chairman laughed, and invited the board to raise their glasses to Chris and Sue Haskins.

"My spies tell me, Chris," added the chairman, "that you are likely to be the next president of our local Rotary."

"Many a slip," said Chris as he lowered his glass, "and certainly not before Sue takes her place on the area committee of the Mothers' Union. Don't be surprised if she ends up as national chairman," he added, with considerable pride.

"So what do you plan to do next?" asked the chairman.

"Take a month's holiday in Portugal," said Chris without hesitation. "After five years of having to make do with the beach at Cleethorpes and a plate of fish and chips, I think we've earned it."

That also would have made a satisfactory conclusion to this tale, had officialdom not stepped in once again; this time with a letter addressed to Mr. and Mrs. Hoskins from the finance director of the Post Office. They found it waiting for them on the mat when they returned from Albufeira.

**Post Office Headquarters,
148 Old Street, London EC1V 9HQ**

Dear Mr. and Mrs. Hoskins,

**The Post Office is in the process of re-evaluating its property portfolio, and to that end, will be making some changes to the status of some of its older establishments.
I therefore have to inform you that the board has come to the reluctant conclusion that we will no longer require two category A status facilities in the Cleethorpes area. While the new High Street branch will continue as a category A post office, Victoria Crescent will be downgraded to category B. In order that you can make the necessary adjustments, we do not propose to bring in these changes until the New Year.**

We look forward to continuing our relationship with you.

Yours sincerely,

Simon Bryant

Finance Director

"Does that mean what I think it means?" said Sue after she had read the letter a second time.

"In simple terms, love," said Chris, "we can never hope to earn back our original investment of two hundred and fifty thousand, even if we go on working for the rest of our lives."

"Then we'll have to put the post office up for sale."

"But who will want to buy it at that price," asked Chris, "once they discover that the business no longer has category A status?"

"The man from Britannia assured us that once we'd paid off the debt it would be worth a million."

"Only while the business has a turnover of five hundred thousand and generates a profit of around eighty thousand a year," said Chris.

"We should take legal advice."

Chris reluctantly agreed, although he wasn't in much doubt what his solicitor's opinion would be. The law, their advocate dutifully advised them, was not on their side, and therefore he wouldn't recommend them to sue the Post Office, as he couldn't guarantee the outcome. "You might well win a moral victory," he said, "but that won't assist your bank balance."

The next decision Chris and Sue made was to put the post office on the market as they wanted to find out if anyone would show an interest. Once again Chris's judgment turned out to be correct: only three couples even bothered to look over the property, and none of them returned for a second viewing once they discovered it was no longer category A status.

"My bet," said Sue, "is that those officials back at headquarters knew only too well they were going to change our status long before they pocketed our money, but it suited them not to tell us."

"You may well be right," said Chris, "but you can be sure of one thing—they won't have put anything in writing at the time, so we would never be able to prove it."

"And neither did we."

"What are you getting at, love?"

"How much have they stolen from us?" demanded Sue.

"Well, if by that you mean our original investment—"

"Our life savings, every penny we've earned over the past thirty years, not to mention our pension."

Chris paused and raised his head, while he made some calculations. "Not including any profit we might have hoped for, once we'd seen our capital returned—"

"Yes, only what they've stolen from us," Sue repeated.

"A little over two hundred and fifty thousand, if you don't include interest," said Chris.

"And we have no hope of seeing a penny of that original investment back, even if we were to work for the rest of our lives?"

"That's about the sum of it, love."

"Then it's my intention to retire on January the first."

"And what are you expecting to live off for the rest of your life?" asked Chris.

"Our original investment."

"And how do you intend to go about that?"

"By taking advantage of our spotless reputation."

The End

Chris and Sue rose early the following morning: after all, they had a lot of work to do during the next three months if they hoped to accumulate enough capital to retire by 1 January. Sue warned Chris that meticulous preparation would be needed if her plan was to succeed. He didn't disagree. They both knew that they couldn't risk pressing the button until the second Friday in November, when they would have a six-week window of opportunity—Chris's expression—before "those people back in London" worked out what they were really up to. But that didn't mean there wasn't a lot of preliminary work to be done in the meantime. To start with, they needed to plan their getaway, even before they set about retrieving any stolen money. Neither considered what they were about to embark on as theft.

Sue unfolded a map of Europe and spread it across the post office counter. They discussed the different alternatives for several days and finally settled on Portugal, which they both considered would be ideal for early retirement. On their many visits to the Algarve they had always returned to Albufeira, the town where they had spent their shortened honeymoon, and revisited on their tenth, twentieth, and many more wedding anniversaries. They had even promised themselves that was where they would retire if they won the lottery.

The next day Sue purchased a tape of *Portuguese for Beginners* which they played before breakfast every morning, and then spent an hour in the evening, testing out their new skills. They were pleased to discover that over the years they had both picked up more of the language than they realized. Although not fluent, they were certainly not beginners. The two of them quickly moved on to the advanced tapes.

"We won't be able to use our own passports," Chris pointed out to his wife while shaving one morning. "We'll have to consider a change of identity, otherwise the authorities would be on to us in no time."

"I've already thought about that," said Sue, "and we should take advantage of working in our own post office."

Chris stopped shaving, and turned to listen to his wife.

"Don't forget, we already supply all the necessary forms for customers who want to obtain passports."

Chris didn't interrupt as Sue went over how she planned to make sure that they could safely leave the country under assumed names.

Chris chuckled. "Perhaps I'll grow a beard," he said, putting his razor down.

Over the years, Chris and Sue had made friends with several customers who regularly shopped at the post office. The two of them wrote down on separate sheets of paper the names of all their customers who fulfilled the criteria Sue was looking for.

They ended up with a list of two dozen candidates: thirteen women and eleven men. From that moment on, whenever one of the unsuspecting regulars entered the shop, Sue or Chris would strike up a conversation that had only one purpose.

"Going away for Christmas this year, are we, Mrs. Brewer?"

"No, Mrs. Haskins, my son and his wife will be joining us on Christmas Eve so that we can get to know our new granddaughter."

"How nice for you, Mrs. Brewer," replied Sue. "Chris and I are thinking of spending Christmas in the States."

"How exciting," said Mrs. Brewer. "I've never even been abroad," she admitted, "let alone America."

Mrs. Brewer had reached the second round, but would not be questioned again until her next visit.

By the end of September, seven other names had joined Mrs. Brewer on the shortlist—four women and three men, all between the ages of fifty-one and fifty-seven, who had only one thing in common: they had never traveled abroad.

The next problem the Haskins faced was

filling in an application for a birth certificate. This required far more detailed questioning, and both Sue and Chris quickly backed off whenever one of the shortlisted candidates showed the slightest sign of suspicion. By the beginning of October they were down to the names of four customers who had unwittingly supplied their date of birth, place of birth, mother's maiden name and father's first name.

The Haskins' next visit was to Boots the chemist in St. Peter's Avenue, where they took turns to sit in a little cubicle and have several strips of photographs taken at £2.50 a time. Sue then set about completing the necessary application forms for a passport, on behalf of four of her unsuspecting customers. She filled in all the relevant details, while enclosing photographs of herself and Chris, along with a postal order for £42. As the postmaster, Chris was only too happy to pen his real signature on the bottom of each form Sue filled in.

The four application forms were posted to the passport office at Petty France in London on the Monday, Thursday, Friday and Saturday of the last week in October.

On Wednesday, 11 November the first

passport arrived back at Victoria Crescent, addressed to Mr. Reg Appleyard. Two days later, a second appeared, for Mrs. Audrey Ramsbottom. The following day Mrs. Betty Brewer's turned up, and finally, a week later, Mr. Stan Gerrard's.

Sue had already pointed out to Chris that they would have to leave the country using one set of passports, which they would then need to discard, before they switched to the second pair, but not until they had found somewhere to live in Albufeira.

Chris and Sue continued to practice their Portuguese whenever they were alone in the shop, while informing any regulars that

they would be away over the Christmas period as they were planning a trip to America.
The inquisitive were rewarded with such details as a week in San Francisco, followed
by a few days in Seattle.

By the second week in November, everything was in place to press the button for
Operation Money Back Guaranteed.

At nine o'clock on Friday morning Sue
made her weekly phone call to headquarters. She entered her personal code before
being transferred to forward finance. The
only difference this time was that she could
hear her heart beating. Sue repeated her
code before informing the credit officer how
much cash she would require for the following week—an amount large enough to allow
her to cover withdrawals for any post office
savings accounts, pensions and cashed
postal orders. Although an accountant from
headquarters always checked the books at
the end of every month, considerable lee-
way was allowed in the run-up to Christmas. A demanding audit was then carried
out in January to make sure the books bal-

anced, but neither Chris nor Sue had any intention of being around in January. For the past six years Sue's books had always balanced, and she was considered by headquarters to be a model manager.

Sue had to check the records to remind herself of the amount she had requested in the same week of the previous year—£40,000, which had turned out to be £800 more than she needed. This year she asked for £60,000, and waited for some comment from the credit officer, but the voice from headquarters sounded neither surprised nor concerned. The full amount was delivered by a security van the following Monday.

During the week Chris and Sue fulfilled all their customers' obligations; after all, it had never been their intention to short-change any of their regulars, but they still found themselves with a surplus of £21,000 at the end of week one. They left the cash—used notes only—locked up in the safe, just in case some fastidious official from headquarters decided to carry out a spot-check.

Once Sue had closed the front door at six o'clock and pulled down the blinds, the two of them would only converse in Portuguese, while they spent the rest of the evening filling in postal orders, rubbing out scratch cards and entering lottery numbers, often falling asleep as they worked.

Every morning Chris would rise early and climb into his aging Rover, with Stamps as his only companion. He traveled north, east, south and west—Monday Lincoln, Tuesday Louth, Wednesday Skegness, Thursday Hull and Friday Immingham, where he would cash several postal orders, and also collect his winnings on the scratch cards and lottery tickets, enabling him to supplement their newly acquired savings with an extra few hundred pounds each day.

On the last Friday in November, week two, Sue applied for £70,000 from head office, so that by the following Saturday, they were able to add a further £32,000 to their invisible earnings.

On the first Friday in December, Sue raised the stakes to £80,000, and was surprised to discover that there were still no questions back at headquarters: after all, hadn't Sue Haskins been manager of the year, with a special commendation from the board? A security van dutifully delivered the full amount in cash early on the Monday morning.

Another week of increased profits allowed Sue Haskins to add a further £39,000 to the pot without any of the other players round the table demanding to see her hand. They were now showing a surplus of well over £100,000, which was stacked up in neat little piles of used notes, resting on top of the four passports buried at the bottom of the safe.

Chris hardly slept at night as he continued to sign countless postal orders, rub out piles of scratch cards and, before going to bed, fill in numerous lottery tickets with endless combinations. By day he visited every post office within a fifty-mile radius, gathering his spoils, but, despite his dedication, by the second week in December Mr. and Mrs. Haskins had only collected just over half the amount required to retrieve the £250,000 they had originally invested.

Sue warned Chris that they would have to take an even bigger risk if they still hoped to acquire the full amount by Christmas Eve.

On the second Friday in December, week four, Sue called the issuing manager at headquarters, and made a request for £115,000.

"You're having a busy Christmas," suggested a voice on the other end of the line.

First sign of any suspicion, thought Sue, but she had her script well prepared.

"Run off my feet," Sue told him, "but don't forget, more people retire to Cleethorpes than any other seaside town in Britain."

"You learn something new every day," came back the voice on the other end of the line, before adding, "Don't worry, the cash will be with you on Monday. Keep up the good work."

"I will," promised Sue, and, emboldened by the exchange, requested £140,000 for the final week before Christmas, aware that any sum above £150,000 was always referred back to head office in London.

When Sue pulled down the blinds at six o'clock on Christmas Eve, both of them were exhausted.

Sue was the first to recover. "We haven't a moment to waste," she reminded her husband as she walked across to the bulging safe. She entered the code, pulled open the door and withdrew everything from their current account. She then placed the money on the counter in neat bundles— fifties, twenties, tens and fives—before they set about counting their spoils.

Chris checked the final figure and confirmed that they were £267,300 in credit. They put £17,300 back in the safe, and locked the door. After all, they had never intended to make a profit—that would be stealing. Sue began to put elastic bands around each thousand, while Chris transferred the two hundred and fifty bundles carefully into an old RAF duffel bag. By eight o'clock they were ready to leave. Chris set the alarm, slipped quietly out of the back door and placed the duffel bag in the boot of their Rover, on top of four other cases his wife had packed earlier that morning. Sue joined him in the front of the car, as Chris turned on the ignition.

"We've forgotten something," said Sue as she pulled the door closed.

"Stamps," they said in unison. Chris turned off the ignition, got out of the car and returned to the post office. He re-entered the code, switched off the alarm and opened the back door in search of Stamps. He found him fast asleep in the kitchen, reluctant to be enticed out of his warm basket and into the back seat of the car. Didn't they realize it was Christmas Eve?

Chris reset the alarm and locked the door for a second time.

At eight-nineteen p.m. Mr. and Mrs. Haskins set out on the journey for Ashford in Kent. Sue worked out that they had four clear days before anyone would be aware of their absence. Christmas Day, Boxing Day, Sunday, Monday (a bank holiday), back in theory on Tuesday morning, by which time they would be viewing properties in the Algarve.

The two of them hardly spoke a word on the long journey to Kent, not even in Portuguese. Sue couldn't believe they'd gone through with it, and Chris was even more surprised that they'd got away with it.

"We haven't yet," Sue reminded him, "not until we drive into Albufeira, and don't forget, Mr. Appleyard, we no longer have the same names."

"Living in sin after all these years are we, Mrs. Brewer?"

Chris brought the car to a halt outside their daughter's home just after midnight. Tracey opened the front door to greet her mother, while Chris removed one of the suitcases and the duffel bag from the boot.

Tracey had never seen her parents looking so exhausted, and felt they had aged since she'd last seen them in the summer. Perhaps it was just the long journey. Tracey took them through to the kitchen, sat them both down and made them a cup of tea. They hardly spoke, and when Tracey eventually bundled them off to bed, her father wouldn't allow her to carry the old duffel bag up to the guest bedroom.

Sue woke every time she heard a car come to a halt in the street outside, wondering if it was marked with the bold fluorescent lettering POLICE. Chris waited for the front-door bell to ring before someone came bounding up the stairs to drag the duffel bag from under the bed, arrest them and escort them both to the nearest police station.

After a sleepless night they joined Tracey in the kitchen for breakfast.

"Happy Christmas," said Tracey, before kissing them both on the cheek. Neither of them responded. Had they forgotten it was Christmas Day? They both looked embarrassed as they stared at the two wrapped boxes that their daughter had placed on the table. They hadn't remembered to buy

Tracey a Christmas present and resorted to giving her cash, something they hadn't done since she was a teenager. Tracey hoped that it was nothing more than the Christmas rush, and excitement at the thought of their visit to the States, which had caused such uncharacteristic behavior.

Boxing Day turned out to be a little better. Sue and Chris appeared more relaxed, although they often lapsed into long silences. After lunch Tracy suggested that they take Stamps for a run across the Downs and get some fresh air. During the long walk one of them would begin a sentence and then fall silent. A few minutes later the other would finish it.

By Sunday morning Tracey felt that they both looked a lot better, even chatting away about their trip to America. But two things puzzled her. When she saw her parents coming down the stairs carrying the duffel bag with Stamps in their wake, she could have sworn they were speaking Portuguese. And why bother to take Stamps to America, when she had already offered to take care of the dog while they were away?

The next surprise came when they set off for Heathrow after breakfast. When her father packed the duffel bag and their suitcase into the boot of the car, she was surprised to see three large bags already in the boot. Why bother with so much luggage when they were only going away for a fortnight?

Tracey stood on the pavement and waved goodbye, as her parents' car trundled off down the road. When the old Rover reached the end of the street it swung right, instead of left, which took them in the opposite direction to Heathrow. Something was wrong. Tracey dismissed the mistake, aware that they could correct their error long before they reached the motorway.

Once Chris and Sue had joined the motorway, they followed the signs for Dover. The two of them became more and more nervous as each minute passed, aware that there was now no turning back. Only Stamps seemed to be enjoying the adventure as he stared out of the back window wagging his tail.

Once again, Mr. Appleyard and Mrs. Brewer went over their plan. When they reached the docks, Sue would jump out of the car and join the queue of foot passengers waiting to board, while Chris drove the

Rover up the car ramp and on to the ferry. They agreed not to meet again until the boat had docked in Calais and Chris had driven on to the dockside.

Sue stood at the bottom of the gangway and waited nervously at the back of the queue as she watched their Rover edge toward the entrance of the hold. Her heart raced when she saw a customs officer double-check Chris's passport, and invite him to step out of the car and stand to one side. She had to stop herself from running across so she could overhear their conversation—she couldn't risk it now they were no longer married.

"Good morning, Mr. Appleyard," said the customs officer, and then added after looking in the back of the car, "were you hoping to take the dog abroad with you?"

"Oh yes," replied Chris. "We never travel anywhere without Stamps."

The customs official studied Mr. Appleyard's passport more carefully. "But you don't have the necessary documents to take a dog abroad with you."

Chris felt beads of sweat running down his forehead. Stamps's papers were still attached to the passport of Mr. Haskins,

which he had left in the safe back at Cleethorpes.

"Oh hell," said Chris. "I must have left
them at home."

"Bad luck, sir. I hope you don't have far to
travel because there isn't another ferry until
this time tomorrow."

Chris glanced helplessly across at his
wife, before climbing back into the car. He
looked down at Stamps, who was sleeping
soundly on the back seat, oblivious to the
problem he was causing. Chris swung the
car round and joined an overwrought Sue,
who was waiting impatiently to find out why
he hadn't been allowed to board. Once
Chris had explained the problem, all she
said was, "We can't risk returning to
Cleethorpes."

"I agree," said Chris, "we'll have to go
back to Ashford, and hope we can find a vet
that's open on a bank holiday."

"That wasn't part of our plan," said Sue.

"I know," said Chris, "but I'm not willing
to leave Stamps behind." Sue nodded in
agreement.

Chris swung the Rover onto the main
road, and began the journey back to Ashford. Mr. and Mrs. Haskins arrived just in

time to join their daughter for lunch. Tracey was delighted that her parents were able to spend a couple more days with her, but she still couldn't understand why they weren't willing to leave Stamps with her; after all, it wasn't as if they were going away for the rest of their lives.

Chris and Sue spent another uncommunicative day and a further sleepless night in Ashford. A duffel bag containing a quarter of a million pounds was tucked under the bed.

On Monday a local vet kindly agreed to give Stamps all the necessary injections. He then attached a certificate to Mr. Appleyard's passport, but not in time for them to catch the last ferry.

The Haskins didn't sleep a wink on the Monday night, and by the time the street lights went out the following morning, they both knew they could no longer go through with it. They lay awake, preparing a new plan—in English.

Chris and Sue finally left their daughter after breakfast the following morning. They drove to the end of the road and this time, to Tracey's relief, turned left, not right, and headed back in the direction of Cleethorpes. By the time they'd swept past the Heathrow exit, their revised plan was in place.

"The moment we arrive home," said Sue, "we'll put all the money back in the safe."

"How will we explain having that amount of cash, when the Post Office accountant carries out his annual audit next month?" asked Chris.

"By the time they get around to checking what's left in the safe, as long as we don't apply for any more money, we should have been able to dispose of most of the cash simply by carrying out our regular transactions."

"What about the postal orders that we've already cashed?"

"There's still enough cash left in the safe to cover them," Sue reminded her husband.

"But the scratch cards and the lottery tickets?"

"We'll have to make up the difference from our own money—that way they'll end up none the wiser."

"I agree," said Chris, sounding relieved for the first time in days, and then he remembered the passports.

"We'll destroy them," said Sue, "as soon as we get home."

By the time the Haskins had crossed the Lincolnshire border, they had made up their minds to continue running the post office, despite its diminished status. Sue had already come up with several ideas for extra items they could sell over the counter, while making the best of what was left of their franchise.

A smile settled on Sue's lips when Chris finally turned into Victoria Crescent, a smile that was quickly removed when she saw the flashing blue lights. When the old Rover came to a halt, a dozen policemen surrounded the car.

"Oh shit," said Sue. Extreme language for the chairman of the Mothers' Union, thought Chris, but on balance, he had to agree with her.

Mr. and Mrs. Haskins were arrested on the evening of 29 December. They were driven to Cleethorpes police station and placed in separate interview rooms. There was no need for the local police to conduct a good cop, bad cop routine, as both of them confessed immediately. They spent the night in separate cells, and the following morning they were charged with the theft of £250,000, being the property of the Post Office, and obtaining, by deception, four passports.

They pleaded guilty to both charges.

Sue Haskins was released from Moreton Hall after serving four months of her sentence. Chris joined her a year later.

While he was in prison Chris worked on another plan. However, when he was released Britannia Finance didn't feel able to back him. To be fair, Mr. Tremaine had retired.

Mr. and Mrs. Haskins sold their property on Victoria Crescent for £100,000. A week later they climbed into their ancient Rover and drove off to Dover, where they boarded the ferry after presenting the correct passports. Once they had found a suitable location on the seafront in Albufeira, they opened a fish-and-chip shop. Haskins' hasn't caught on with the locals yet, but with a hundred thousand Brits visiting the Algarve every year, there's proved to be no shortage of customers.

I was among those who risked a small investment in the new enterprise, and I am happy to report that I have recouped every penny with interest. Funny old world. But then as Mr. Justice Gray observed, Mr. and Mrs. Haskins were not criminals.

Only one footnote. Stamps died while Sue and Chris were in prison.

Maestro

The Italians are the only race I know who have the ability to serve without appearing subservient. The French will happily spill sauce all over your favorite tie, with no hint of an apology, at the same time cursing you in their native tongue. The Chinese don't speak to you at all, and the Greeks think nothing of leaving you alone for an hour before they even offer you a menu. The Americans are at pains to let you know that they aren't really waiters at all, but out-of-work actors, who then proceed to recite the specials on the menu as if performing for an audition. The English are quite likely to engage you in a long conversation, leaving an impression that you ought to be having dinner with them, rather than your guest, and as for the Germans . . . well, when did you last eat at a German restaurant?

So it is left to the Italians to sweep the board and gather up the crumbs. They combine the charm of the Irish, the culinary expertise of the French and the thoroughness of the Swiss, and despite their ability to produce a bill that never seems to add up, we allow them to go on fleecing us.

This was certainly true of Mario Gambotti.

Mario came from a long line of Florentines who could not sing, paint or play football, so he happily joined his fellow exiles in London, where he began an apprenticeship in the restaurant business.

Whenever I go to his fashionable little restaurant in Fulham for lunch, he somehow manages to hide his disapproval when I order minestrone soup, spaghetti Bolognese and a bottle of Chianti classico.

"What an excellent choice, maestro," he declares, not bothering to scribble down my order on his pad. Please note "maestro": not my lord, which would be sycophantic, not sir, which would be ridiculous after twenty years of friendship, but maestro, a particularly flattering sobriquet, as I have it on good authority (his wife) that he has never read one of my books.

When I was in attendance at North Sea Camp open prison, Mario wrote to the governor and suggested that he might be allowed to come down one Friday and cook lunch for me. The governor was amused by the request, and wrote a formal reply, explaining that should he grant the boon, it would not only break several penal regulations, but undoubtedly stir the tabloids into a frenzy of headlines. When the governor showed me a copy of his reply, I was surprised to see that he had signed the letter, *yours ever, Michael.*

"Are you also a customer of Mario's?" I inquired.

"No," replied the governor, "but he has been a customer of mine."

Mario's can be found on the Fulham Road in Chelsea, and the restaurant's popularity is due in no small part to his wife, Teresa, who runs the kitchen. Mario always remains front of house. I regularly have lunch there on a Friday, often accompanied by my two sons and their latest girlfriends, who used to change more often than the menu.

Over the years I have become aware that many of the customers are regulars, which leaves an impression that we are all part of an exclusive club, in which it's almost impossible to book a table unless you are a member. However, the real proof of Mario's popularity is that the restaurant does not accept credit cards—checks, cash and account-paying customers are all welcome, but **NO CREDIT CARDS** is printed in bold letters at the foot of every menu.

During the month of August the establishment is closed, in order for the Gambotti family to return to their native Florence and reunite with all the other Gambottis.

Mario is quintessentially Italian. His red Ferrari can be seen parked outside the restaurant, his yacht—my son James assures me—is moored in Monte Carlo, and his children, Tony, Maria and Roberto, are being educated at St. Paul's, Cheltenham and Summer Fields respectively. After all, it is important that they mix with the sort of people they will be expected to fleece at some time in the future. And whenever I see them at the opera—Verdi and Puccini, never Wagner or Weber—they are always seated in their own box.

So, I hear you ask, how did such a shrewd and intelligent man end up serving at Her Majesty's pleasure? Was he involved in some fracas following a football match between Arsenal and Fiorentina? Did he drive over the speed limit once too often in that Ferrari of his? Perhaps he forgot to pay his poll tax? None of the above. He broke an English law with an action that in the land of his forefathers would be considered no more than an acceptable part of everyday life.

Enter Mr. Dennis Cartwright, who worked for another of Her Majesty's establishments.

Mr. Cartwright was an inspector with the Inland Revenue. He rarely ate out at a restaurant, and certainly not one as exclusive as Mario's. Whenever he and his wife Doris "went Italian," it was normally Pizza Express. However, he took a great interest in Mr. Gambotti, and in how he could possibly maintain such a lifestyle on the amount he was declaring to his local tax office. After all, the restaurant was showing a profit of a mere £172,000, on a turnover of just over two million. So, after tax, Mr. Gambotti was only taking home—Dennis carefully checked the figures—just over £100,000. With a home in Chelsea, three children at private schools and a Ferrari to maintain, not to mention the yacht moored in Monte Carlo, and heaven knows what else in Florence, how did he manage it? Mr. Cartwright, a determined man, was determined to find out.

The tax inspector checked all the figures in Mario's books, and he had to admit they balanced and, what's more, Mr. Gambotti always paid his taxes on time. However, Mr. Cartwright wasn't in any doubt that Mr. Gambotti had to be siphoning off large sums of cash, but how? He must have missed something. Cartwright leaped up in the middle of the night and shouted out loud, *"No credit cards."* He woke his wife.

The next morning, Cartwright went over the books yet again; he was right. There were no credit-card entries. Although all the checks were properly accounted for, and all the customers' accounts tallied, when you considered that there were no credit-card entries, the small amount of cash declared seemed completely out of proportion to the overall takings.

Mr. Cartwright didn't need to be told that his masters would not allow him to waste much time dining at Mario's in order to resolve the mystery of how Mr. Gambotti was salting away such large sums of money. Mr. Buchanan, his supervisor, reluctantly agreed to allow Dennis an advance of £200 to try to discover what was happening on the inside—every penny was to be accounted for—and he only agreed to this after Dennis had pointed out that if he was able to gather enough evidence to put Mr. Gambotti behind bars, imagine just how many other restaurateurs might feel obliged to start declaring their true incomes.

Mr. Cartwright was surprised that it took him a month to book a table at Mario's, and it was only after several calls, always made from home, that he finally was able to secure a reservation. He asked his wife Doris to join him, hoping it would appear less suspicious than if he was sitting on his own, compiling notes. His supervisor agreed with the ploy, but told Dennis that he would have to cover his wife's half of the bill, at his own expense.

"It never crossed my mind to do otherwise," Dennis assured his supervisor.

During a meal of Tuscan bean soup and gnocchi—he was hoping to pay more than one visit to Mario's—Dennis kept a wary eye on his host as he circled the different tables, making small talk and attending to his customers' slightest whims. His wife couldn't help but notice that Dennis seemed distracted, but she decided not to comment, as it was a rare occurrence for her husband to invite her out for a meal, other than on her birthday.

Mr. Cartwright began committing to memory that there were thirty-nine tables dotted around the restaurant (he double-checked) and roughly a hundred and twenty

covers. He also observed, by taking time over his coffee, that Mario managed two sittings on several of the tables. He was impressed by how quickly three waiters could clear a table, replace the cloth and napkins, and moments later make it appear as if no one had ever been sitting there.

When Mario presented Mr. Cartwright with his bill, he paid in cash and insisted on a receipt. When they left the restaurant,

Doris drove them both home, which allowed Dennis to write down all the relevant figures in his little book while they still remained fresh in his memory.

"What a lovely meal," commented his wife on their journey back to Romford. "I do hope that we'll be able to go there again some time."

"We will, Doris," he promised her, "next week." He paused. "If I can get a table."

Mr. and Mrs. Cartwright visited the restaurant again three weeks later, this time for dinner. Dennis was impressed that Mario not only remembered his name, but even seated him at the same table. On this occasion, Mr. Cartwright observed that Mario was able to fit in a pre-theater booking— almost full; an evening sitting—packed out; and a post-theater sitting—half full; while last orders were not taken until eleven o'clock.

Mr. Cartwright estimated that nearly three hundred and fifty customers passed through the restaurant during the evening, and if you added that to the lunchtime clientele, the total came to just over five hundred a day. He also calculated that around half of them were paying cash, but he still had no way of proving it.

Dennis's dinner bill came to £75 (it's fascinating how restaurants appear to charge more in the evening than they do for lunch, even when they serve exactly the same food). Mr. Cartwright estimated that each customer was being charged between £25 and £40, and that was probably on the conservative side. So in any given week, Mario had to be serving at least three thousand customers, returning him an income of around £90,000 a week, which was in excess of four million pounds a year, even if you discounted the month of August.

When Mr. Cartwright returned to his office the following morning, he once again went over the restaurant's books. Mr. Gambotti was declaring a turnover of £2,120,000, and showing, after outgoings, a profit of £172,000. So what was happening to the other two million?

Mr. Cartwright remained baffled. He took the ledgers home in the evening, and continued to study the figures long into the night.

"Eureka," he declared just before putting on his pajamas. One of the outgoings didn't add up. The following morning he made an appointment to see his supervisor. "I'll need to get my hands on the details of these particular weekly numbers," Dennis told Mr. Buchanan, as he placed a forefinger on one of the items listed under outgoings, "and more important," he added, "without Mr. Gambotti realizing what I'm up to." Mr. Buchanan sanctioned a request for him to be out of the office, as long as it didn't require any further visits to Mario's.

Mr. Cartwright spent most of the weekend refining his plan, aware that just the slightest hint of what he was up to would allow Mr. Gambotti enough time to cover his tracks.

On Monday Mr. Cartwright rose early and drove to Fulham, not bothering to check in at the office. He parked his Skoda down a side street that allowed him a clear view of the entrance to Mario's restaurant. He removed a notebook from an inside pocket and began to write down the names of every tradesman who visited the premises that morning.

The first van to arrive and park on the double yellow line outside the restaurant's front door was a well-known purveyor of vegetables, followed a few minutes later by a master butcher. Next to unload her wares was a fashionable florist, followed by a wine merchant, a fishmonger and finally the one vehicle Mr. Cartwright had been waiting for—a laundry van. Once the driver had unloaded three large crates, dumped them inside the restaurant and come back out, lugging three more crates, he drove away. Mr. Cartwright didn't need to follow the van as the company's name, address and telephone number were emblazoned across both sides of the vehicle.

Mr. Cartwright returned to the office, and was seated behind his desk just before midday. He reported immediately to his supervisor, and sought his authority to make a spot-check on the company concerned. Mr. Buchanan again sanctioned his request, but on this occasion recommended caution. He advised Cartwright to carry out a routine inquiry, so that the company concerned would not work out what he was really looking for. "It may take a little longer," Buchanan added, "but it will give us a far better chance of success in the long run. I'll drop them a line today, and then you can fix up a meeting, at their convenience."

Dennis went along with his supervisor's suggestion, which meant that he didn't turn up at the offices of the Marco Polo laundry company for another three weeks. On arrival at the laundry, by appointment, he made it clear to the manager that his visit was nothing more than a routine check, and he wasn't expecting to find any irregularities.

Dennis spent the rest of the day checking through every one of their customers' accounts, only stopping to make detailed notes whenever he came across an entry for Mario's restaurant. By midday he had gathered all the evidence he needed, but he didn't leave Marco Polo's offices until five, so that no one would become suspicious. When Dennis departed for the day, he assured the manager that he was well satisfied with their book-keeping, and there would be no follow-up. What he didn't tell him was that one of their most important customers would be followed up.

Mr. Cartwright was seated at his desk by eight o'clock the following morning, making sure his report was completed before his boss appeared.

When Mr. Buchanan walked in at five to nine, Dennis leaped up from behind his desk, a look of triumph on his face. He was just about to pass on his news, when the supervisor placed a finger to his lips and indicated that he should follow him through to his office. Once the door was closed, Dennis placed the report on the table and took his boss through the details of his inquiries. He waited patiently while Mr. Buchanan studied the documents and considered their implications. He finally looked up, to indicate that Dennis could now speak.

"This shows," Dennis began, "that every day for the past twelve months Mr. Gambotti has sent out two hundred tablecloths and over five hundred napkins to the Marco

Polo laundry. If you then look at this particular entry," he added, pointing to an open ledger on the other side of the desk, "you will observe that Gambotti is only declaring a hundred and twenty bookings a day, for around three hundred customers." Dennis paused before delivering his accountant's coup de grâce. "Why would you need a further three thousand tablecloths and forty-five thousand napkins to be laundered every year, unless you had another forty-five thousand customers?" he asked. He paused once again. "Because he's laundering money," said Dennis, clearly pleased with his little pun.

"Well done, Dennis," said the head of department. "Prepare a full report and I'll see that it ends up on the desk of our fraud department."

Try as he might, Mario could not explain away 3,000 tablecloths and 45,000 napkins to Mr. Gerald Henderson, his cynical solicitor. The lawyer only had one piece of advice for his client, "Plead guilty, and I'll see if I can make a deal."

The Inland Revenue successfully claimed

back two million pounds in taxes from Mario's restaurant, and the judge sent Mario Gambotti to prison for six months. He ended up only having to serve a four-week sentence—three months off for good behavior and, as it was his first offense, he was put on a tag for two months.

Mr. Henderson, an astute lawyer, even managed to get the trial set in the court calendar for the last week in July. He explained to the presiding judge that it was the only time Mr. Gambotti's eminent QC would be available to appear before his lordship. The date of 30 July was agreed by all parties.

After a week spent in Belmarsh high-security prison in south London, Mario was transferred to North Sea Camp open prison in Lincolnshire, where he completed his sentence. Mario's lawyer had selected the prison on the grounds that he was unlikely to meet up with many of his old customers deep in the fens of Lincolnshire.

Meanwhile, the rest of the Gambotti family flew off to Florence for the month of August, not able fully to explain to the grandmothers why Mario couldn't be with them on this occasion.

Mario was released from North Sea Camp at nine o'clock on Monday, 1 September.

As he walked out of the front gate, he found Tony seated behind the wheel of his Ferrari, waiting to pick his father up. Three hours later Mario was standing at the front door of his restaurant to greet the first customer. Several regulars commented on the fact that he appeared to have lost a few pounds while he'd been away on holiday, while others remarked on how tanned and fit he looked.

Six months after Mario had been released, a newly promoted deputy supervisor decided to carry out another spot-check on Marco Polo's laundry. This time Dennis turned up unannounced. He ran a practiced eye over the books, to find that Mario's was now sending only 120 tablecloths to the laundry each day, along with 300 napkins, despite the fact that the restaurant appeared to be just as popular. How was he managing to get away with it this time?

The following morning Dennis parked his Skoda down a side street off the Fulham Road once again, allowing him an uninter-rupted view of Mario's front door. He felt confident that Mr. Gambotti must now be using more than one laundry service, but to his disappointment the only van to appear and deposit and collect any laundry that day was Marco Polo's.

Mr. Cartwright drove back to Romford at eight that evening, completely baffled. Had he hung around until just after midnight, Dennis would have seen several waiters leaving the restaurant, carrying bulging sports bags with squash racquets poking out of the top. Do you know any Italian waiters who play squash?

Mario's staff were delighted that their wives could earn some extra cash by taking in a little laundry each day, especially as Mr. Gambotti had supplied each of them with a brand-new washing machine.

I booked a table for lunch at Mario's on the Friday after I had been released from prison. He was standing on the doorstep, waiting to greet me, and I was immediately ushered through to my usual table in the corner of the room by the window, as if I had never been away.

Mario didn't bother to offer me a menu because his wife appeared out of the kitchen carrying a large plate of spaghetti, which she placed on the table in front of me. Mario's son Tony followed close behind with a steaming bowl of Bolognese sauce, and his daughter Maria with a large chunk of Parmesan cheese and a grater.

"A bottle of Chianti classico?" suggested Mario, as he removed the cork. "On the house," he insisted.

"Thank you, Mario," I said, and whispered, "by the way, the governor of North Sea Camp asked me to pass on his best wishes."

"Poor Michael," Mario sighed, "what a sad existence. Can you begin to imagine a lifetime spent eating toad-in-the-hole, followed by semolina pudding?" He smiled as he poured me a glass of wine. "Still, maestro, you must have felt quite at home."

Don't Drink the Water

"If you want to murder someone," said Karl, "don't do it in England."

"Why not?" I asked innocently.

"The odds are against you getting away with it," my fellow inmate warned me, as we continued to walk round the exercise yard. "You've got a much better chance in Russia."

"I'll try to remember that," I assured him.

"Mind you," added Karl, "I knew a countryman of yours who did get away with murder, but at some cost."

* * *

It was Association, that welcome 45-minute break when you're released from your cell. You can either spend your time on the ground floor, which is about the size of a basketball court, sitting around chatting, playing table tennis or watching television, or you can go out into the fresh air and stroll around the perimeter of the yard—about the size of a football pitch. Despite being surrounded by a twenty-foot-high concrete wall topped with razor wire, and with only the sky to look up at, this was, for me, the highlight of the day.

While I was incarcerated at Belmarsh, a category A high-security prison in southeast London, I was locked in my cell for twenty-three hours a day (think about it). You are let out only to go to the canteen to pick up your lunch (five minutes), which you then eat in your cell. Five hours later you collect your supper (five more minutes), when they also hand you tomorrow's breakfast in a plastic bag so that they don't have to let you out again before lunch the following day. The only other blessed release is Association, and even that can be canceled if the prison is short-staffed (which happens about twice a week).

I always used the 45-minute escape to

power-walk, for two reasons: one, I needed the exercise because on the outside I attend a local gym five days a week, and, two, not many prisoners bothered to try and keep up with me. Karl was the exception.

Karl was a Russian by birth who hailed from that beautiful city of St. Petersburg. He was a contract killer who had just begun a 22-year sentence for disposing of a fellow countryman who was proving tiresome to one of the Mafia gangs back home. He cut his victims up into small pieces, and put what was left of them into an incinerator. Incidentally, his fee—should you want someone disposed of—was five thousand pounds.

Karl was a bear of a man, six foot two and built like a weight-lifter. He was covered in tattoos and never stopped talking. On balance, I didn't consider it wise to interrupt his flow. Like so many prisoners, Karl didn't talk about his own crime, and the golden rule—should you ever end up inside—is never ask what a prisoner is in for, unless they raise the subject. However, Karl did tell me a tale about an Englishman he'd come across in St. Petersburg, which he claimed to have witnessed in the days when he'd been a driver for a government minister.

Although Karl and I were resident on different blocks, we met up regularly for Association. But it still took several perambulations of the yard before I squeezed out of him the story of Richard Barnsley.

DON'T DRINK THE WATER. Richard Barnsley stared at the little plastic card that had been placed on the washbasin in his bathroom. Not the kind of warning you expect to find when you're staying in a five-star hotel, unless, of course, you're in St. Petersburg. By the side of the notice stood two bottles of Evian water. When Dick strolled back into his spacious bedroom, he found two more bottles had been placed on each side of the double bed, and another two on a table by the window. The management weren't taking any chances.

Dick had flown into St. Petersburg to close a deal with the Russians. His company had been selected to build a pipeline that would stretch from the Urals to the Red Sea, a project that several other, more established, companies had tendered for. Dick's firm had been awarded the contract, against considerable odds, but those odds had shortened once he guaranteed Anatol

Chenkov, the Minister for Energy and close personal friend of the President, two million dollars a year for the rest of his life—the only currencies the Russians trade in are dollars and death—especially when the money is going to be deposited in a numbered account.

Before Dick had started up his own company, Barnsley Construction, he had learned his trade working in Nigeria for Bechtel, in Brazil for McAlpine and in Saudi Arabia for Hanover, so along the way he had picked up a trick or two about bribery. Most international companies treat the practice simply as another form of tax, and make the necessary provision for it whenever they present their tender. The secret is always to know how much to offer the minister, and how little to dispose of among his acolytes.

Anatol Chenkov, a Putin appointee, was a tough negotiator, but then under a former regime he had been a major in the KGB. However, when it came to setting up a bank account in Switzerland, the minister was clearly a novice. Dick took full advantage of this; after all, Chenkov had never traveled beyond the Russian border before he was appointed to the Politburo. Dick flew him to

Geneva for the weekend, while he was on an official visit to London for trade talks. He opened a numbered account for him with Picket & Co, and deposited $100,000—seed money—but more than Chenkov had been paid in his lifetime. This sweetener was to ensure that the umbilical cord would last for the necessary nine months until the contract was signed; a contract that would allow Dick to retire—on far more than two million a year.

Dick returned to the hotel that morning after his final meeting with the minister, having seen him every day for the past week, sometimes publicly, more often privately. It was no different when Chenkov visited London. Neither man trusted the other, but then Dick never felt at ease with anyone who was willing to take a bribe because there was always someone else happy to offer him another percentage point. However, Dick felt more confident this time, as both of them seemed to have signed up for the same retirement policy.

Dick also helped to cement the relationship with a few added extras that Chenkov quickly became accustomed to. A Rolls-Royce would always pick him up at Heathrow and drive him to the Savoy Hotel. On arrival, he would be shown to his usual riverside suite, and women appeared every evening as regularly as the morning papers. He preferred two of both, one broadsheet, one tabloid.

When Dick checked out of the St. Petersburg hotel half an hour later, the minister's BMW was parked outside the front door waiting to take him to the airport. As he climbed into the back seat, he was surprised to find Chenkov waiting for him. They had parted after their morning meeting just an hour before.

"Is there a problem, Anatol?" he asked anxiously.

"On the contrary," said Chenkov. "I have just had a call from the Kremlin which I didn't feel we should discuss over the phone, or even in my office. The President will be visiting St. Petersburg on the sixteenth of May and has made it clear that he wishes to preside over the signing ceremony."

"But that gives us less than three weeks to complete the contract," said Dick.

"You assured me at our meeting this morning," Chenkov reminded him, "that there were only a few *i*s to dot and *t*s to cross—an expression I'd not come across before—before you'd be able to finalize the contract." The minister paused and lit his first cigar of the day before adding, "With that in mind, my dear friend, I look forward to seeing you back in St. Petersburg in three weeks' time." Chenkov's statement sounded casual, whereas, in truth, it had taken almost three years for the two men to reach this stage, and now it would only be another three weeks before the deal was finally sealed.

Dick didn't respond as he was already thinking about what needed to be done the moment his plane touched down at Heathrow.

"What's the first thing you'll do after the deal has been signed?" asked Chenkov, breaking into his thoughts.

"Put in a tender for the sanitation contract in this city, because whoever gets it would surely make an even larger fortune."

The minister looked round sharply. "Never raise that subject in public," he said gravely. "It's a very sensitive issue."

Dick remained silent.

"And take my advice, don't drink the water. Last year we lost countless numbers of our citizens who contracted . . ." the minister hesitated, unwilling to add credence to a story that had been splashed across the front pages of every Western paper.

"How many is countless?" inquired Dick.

"None," replied the minister. "Or at least that's the official statistic released by the Ministry of Tourism," he added as the car came to a halt on a double red line outside the entrance of Pulkovo II airport. He leaned forward. "Karl, take Mr. Barnsley's bags to check-in, while I wait here."

Dick leaned across and shook hands with the minister for the second time that morning. "Thank you, Anatol, for everything," he said. "See you in three weeks' time."

"Long life and happiness, my friend," said Chenkov as Dick stepped out of the car.

Dick checked in at the departure desk an hour before boarding was scheduled for his flight to London.

"This is the last call for Flight 902 to London Heathrow," came crackling over the tannoy.

"Is there another flight going to London right now?" asked Dick.

"Yes," replied the man behind the check-in desk. "Flight 902 has been delayed, but they're just about to close the gate."

"Can you get me on it?" asked Dick, as he slid a thousand-rouble note across the counter.

Dick's plane touched down at Heathrow three and a half hours later. Once he'd retrieved his case from the carousel, he pushed his trolley through the Nothing to Declare channel and emerged into the arrivals hall.

Stan, his driver, was already waiting among a group of chauffeurs, most of whom were holding up name cards. As soon as Stan spotted his boss, he walked quickly across and relieved him of his suitcase and overnight bag.

"Home or the office?" Stan asked as they walked toward the short-stay carpark.

Dick checked his watch: just after four. "Home," he said. "I'll work in the back of the car."

* * *

Once Dick's Jaguar had emerged from the carpark to begin the journey to Virginia Water, Dick immediately called his office.

"Richard Barnsley's office," said a voice.

"Hi, Jill, it's me. I managed to catch an earlier flight, and I'm on my way home. Is there anything I should be worrying about?"

"No, everything's running smoothly this end," Jill replied. "We're all just waiting to find out how things went in St. Petersburg."

"Couldn't have gone better. The minister wants me back on May sixteenth to sign the contract."

"But that's less than three weeks away."

"Which means we'll all have to get a move on. So set up a board meeting for early next week, and then make an appointment for me to see Sam Cohen first thing tomorrow morning. I can't afford any slip-ups at this stage."

"Can I come to St. Petersburg with you?"

"Not this time, Jill, but once the contract has been signed block out ten days in the diary. Then I'll take you somewhere a little warmer than St. Petersburg."

Dick sat silently in the back of the car, going over everything that needed to be covered before he returned to St. Petersburg. By the time Stan drove through the wrought-iron gates and came to a halt outside the neo-Georgian mansion, Dick knew what had to be done. He jumped out of the car and ran into the house. He left Stan to unload the bags, and his housekeeper to unpack them. Dick was surprised not to find his wife standing on the top step, waiting to greet him, but then he remembered that he'd caught an earlier flight, and Maureen wouldn't be expecting him back for at least another couple of hours.

Dick ran upstairs to his bedroom, and quickly stripped off his clothes, dropping them in a pile on the floor. He went into the bathroom and turned on the shower, allowing the warm jets of water to slowly remove the grime of St. Petersburg and Aeroflot.

After he'd put on some casual clothes, Dick checked his appearance in the mirror. At fifty-three, his hair was turning prematurely gray, and although he tried to hold his stomach in, he knew he ought to lose a few pounds, just a couple of notches on his belt—once the deal was signed and he had a little more time, he promised himself.

He left the bedroom and went down to

the kitchen. He asked the cook to prepare him a salad, and then strolled into the drawing room, picked up *The Times,* and glanced at the headlines. A new leader of the Tory Party, a new leader of the Liberal Democrats, and now Gordon Brown had been elected leader of the Labor Party. None of the major political parties would be fighting the next election under the same leader.

Dick looked up when the phone began to ring. He walked across to his wife's writing desk and picked up the receiver, to hear Jill's voice on the other end of the line.

"The board meeting is fixed for next Thursday at ten o'clock, and I've also arranged for you to see Sam Cohen in his office at eight tomorrow morning." Dick removed a pen from an inside pocket of his blazer. "I've emailed every member of the board to warn them that it's a priority," she added.

"What time did you say my meeting was with Sam?"

"Eight o'clock at his office. He has to be in court by ten for another client."

"Fine." Dick opened his wife's drawer and grabbed the first piece of paper available. He wrote down, *Sam, office, 8, Thur board mtg, 10.* "Well done, Jill," he added. "Better book me back into the Grand Palace Hotel, and email the minister to warn him what time I'll be arriving."

"I already have," Jill replied, "and I've also booked you on a flight to St. Petersburg on the Sunday afternoon."

"Well done. See you around ten tomorrow." Dick put the phone down, and strolled through to his study, with a large smile on his face. Everything was going to plan.

When he reached his desk, Dick transferred the details of his appointments to his diary. He was just about to drop the piece of paper into a wastepaper basket when he decided just to check and see if it contained anything important. He unfolded a letter, which he began to read. His smile turned to a frown, long before he'd reached the final paragraph. He started to read the letter, marked private and personal, a second time.

Dear Mrs. Barnsley,

This is to confirm your appointment at our office on Friday, 30 April, when we will continue our

**discussions on the matter you
raised with me last Tuesday.
Remembering the full implications
of your decision, I have asked my
senior partner to join us on this
occasion.**

   **We both look forward to seeing
you on the 30th.**

   Yours sincerely,

   Andrew Symonds

Dick immediately picked up the phone on
his desk, and dialed Sam Cohen's number,
hoping he hadn't already left for the day.
When Sam pick up his private line, all Dick
said was, "Have you come across a lawyer
called Andrew Symonds?"

   "Only by reputation," said Sam, "but then
I don't specialize in divorce."

   "Divorce?" said Dick, as he heard a car
coming up the gravel driveway. He glanced
out of the window to see a Volkswagen
swing round the circle and come to a halt
outside the front door. Dick watched as
his wife climbed out of her car. "I'll see you
at eight tomorrow, Sam, and the Russian

contract won't be the only thing on the agenda."

Dick's driver dropped him outside Sam Cohen's office in Lincoln's Inn Field a few minutes before eight the following morning. The senior partner rose to greet his client as he entered the room. He gestured to a comfortable chair on the other side of the desk.

Dick had opened his briefcase even before he'd sat down. He took out the letter and passed it across to Sam. The lawyer read it slowly, before placing it on the desk in front of him.

"I've thought about the problem overnight," said Sam, "and I've also had a word with Anna Rentoul, our divorce partner. She's confirmed that Symonds only handles matrimonial disputes, and with that in mind, I'm sorry to say that I'll have to ask you some fairly personal questions."

Dick nodded without comment.

"Have you ever discussed divorce with Maureen?"

"No," said Dick firmly. "We've had rows from time to time, but then what couples who've been together for over twenty years haven't?"

"No more than that?"

"She once threatened to leave me, but I thought that was all in the past." Dick paused. "I'm only surprised that she hasn't raised the subject with me, before consulting a lawyer."

"That's all too common," said Sam. "Over half the husbands who are served with a divorce petition claim they never saw it coming."

"I certainly fall into that category," admitted Dick. "So what do I do next?"

"Not a lot you can do before she serves the writ, and I can't see that there's anything to be gained by raising the subject yourself. After all, nothing may come of it. However, that doesn't mean we shouldn't prepare ourselves. Now, what grounds could she have for divorce?"

"None that I can think of."

"Are you having an affair?"

"No. Well, yes, a fling with my secretary—but it's not going anywhere. She thinks it's serious, but I plan to replace her once the pipeline contract is signed."

"So the deal is still on course?" said Sam.

"Yes, that's originally why I needed to see you so urgently," replied Dick. "I have to be

back in St. Petersburg for May the sixteenth, when both sides will be signing the
contract." He paused. "And it's going to be
witnessed by President Putin."

"Congratulations," said Sam. "How much
will that be worth to you?"

"Why do you ask?"

"I'm wondering if you're not the only person who's hoping that the deal will go
through."

"Around sixty million—" Dick hesitated—
"for the company."

"And do you still own fifty-one percent of
the shares?"

"Yes, but I could always hide—"

"Don't even think about it," said Sam.
"You won't be able to hide anything if
Symonds is on the case. He'll sniff out every
last penny, like a pig hunting for truffles. And
if the court were to discover that you attempted to deceive them, it would only
make the judge more sympathetic to your
wife." The senior partner paused, looked directly at his client, and repeated, "Don't
even think about it."

"So what should I do?"

"Nothing that will arouse suspicion; go
about your business as usual, as if you have

no idea what she's up to. Meanwhile, I'll fix a consultation with counsel, so at least we'll be better prepared than Mr. Symonds will be anticipating. And one more thing," said Sam, once again looking directly at his client, "no more extra-marital activities until this problem has been resolved. That's an order."

Dick kept a close eye on his wife during the next few days, but she gave no sign of there being anything untoward. If anything, she showed an unusual interest in how the trip to St. Petersburg had gone, and over dinner on Thursday evening even asked if the board had come to a decision.

"They most certainly have," Dick replied emphatically. "Once Sam had taken the directors through each clause, gone over every detail, and answered all of their questions, they virtually rubber-stamped the contract." Dick poured himself a second cup of coffee. He was taken by surprise by his wife's next question.

"Why don't I join you when you go to St. Petersburg? We could fly out on the Friday," she added, "and spend the weekend visiting the Hermitage and the Summer Palace.

We might even find enough time to see Catherine's amber collection—something I've always wanted to do."

Dick didn't reply immediately, aware that this was not a casual suggestion as it had been years since Maureen had accompanied him on a business trip. Dick's first reaction was to wonder what she was up to. "Let me think about it," he eventually responded, leaving his coffee to go cold.

Dick rang Sam Cohen within minutes of arriving at his office and reported the conversation to his lawyer.

"Symonds must have advised her to witness the signing of the contract," suggested Cohen.

"But why?"

"So that Maureen will be able to claim that over the years she has played a leading role in your business success, always being there to support you at those critical moments in your career . . ."

"Balls," said Dick, "she's never taken any interest in how I make my money, only in how she can spend it."

". . . and therefore she must be entitled to fifty percent of your assets."

"But that could amount to over thirty million pounds," Dick protested.

"Symonds has obviously done his homework."

"Then I'll simply tell her that she can't come on the trip. It's not appropriate."

"Which will allow Mr. Symonds to change tack. He'll then portray you as a heartless man, who, the moment you became a success, cut his client out of your life, often traveling abroad, accompanied by a secretary who—"

"OK, OK, I get the picture. So allowing her to come to St. Petersburg might well prove to be the lesser of two evils."

"On the one hand . . ." counseled Sam.

"Bloody lawyers," said Dick before he could finish the sentence.

"Funny how you only need us when you're in trouble," Sam rejoined. "So let's make sure that this time we anticipate her next move."

"And what's that likely to be?"

"Once she's got you to St. Petersburg, she'll want to have sex."

"We haven't had sex for years."

"And not because I haven't wanted to, m'lord."

"Oh, hell," said Dick, "I can't win."

"You can as long as you don't follow Lady Longford's advice—when asked if she had ever considered divorcing Lord Longford, she replied, 'Divorce, never, murder, often.'"

Mr. and Mrs. Richard Barnsley checked into the Grand Palace Hotel in St. Petersburg a fortnight later. A porter placed their bags on a trolley, and then accompanied them to the Tolstoy Suite on the ninth floor.

"Must go to the loo before I burst," said Dick as he rushed into the room ahead of his wife. While her husband disappeared into the bathroom, Maureen looked out of the window and admired the golden domes of St. Nicholas's Cathedral.

Once he'd locked the door, Dick removed the DON'T DRINK THE WATER sign that was perched on the washbasin and tucked it into the back pocket of his trousers. Next he unscrewed the tops of the two Evian bottles and poured the contents down the sink. He then refilled both bottles with tap water, before screwing the tops firmly back on and returning them to their place on the corner of the basin. He unlocked the door and strolled out of the bathroom.

Dick started to unpack his suitcase, but stopped the moment Maureen disappeared into the bathroom. First, he transferred the DON'T DRINK THE WATER sign from his back pocket into the side flap of his suitcase. He zipped up the flap, before checking around the room. There was a small bottle of Evian water on each side of the bed, and two large bottles on the table by the window. He grabbed the bottle by his wife's side of the bed and retreated into the kitchenette at the far end of the room. Dick poured the contents down the sink, and refilled the bottle with tap water. He then returned it to Maureen's side of the bed. Next, he took the two large bottles from the table by the window and repeated the process.

By the time his wife had come out of the bathroom, Dick had almost finished unpacking. While Maureen continued to unpack her suitcase, Dick strolled across to his side of the bed and dialed a number he didn't need to look up. As he waited for the phone to be answered, he opened the bottle of Evian water on his side of the bed, and took a gulp.

"Hi, Anatol, it's Dick Barnsley. I thought

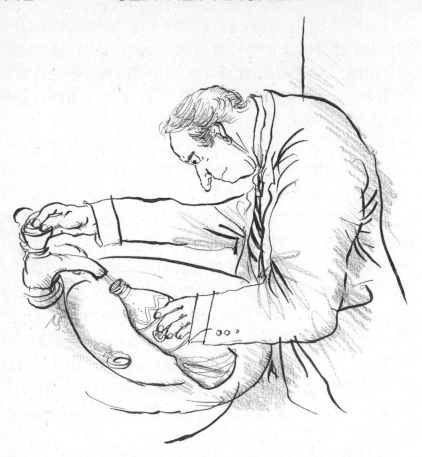

I'd let you know that we've just checked in to the Grand Palace."

"Welcome back to St. Petersburg," said a friendly voice. "And is your wife with you on this occasion?"

"She most certainly is," replied Dick, "and very much looking forward to meeting you."

"Me too," said the minister, "so make

sure that you have a relaxed weekend because everything is set up for Monday
morning. The President is due to fly in tomorrow night so he'll be present when the
contract is signed."

"Ten o'clock at the Winter Palace?"

"Ten o'clock," repeated Chenkov. "I'll
pick you up from your hotel at nine. It's only
a thirty-minute drive, but we can't afford to
be late for this one."

"I'll be waiting for you in the lobby," said
Dick. "See you then." He put the phone
down and turned to his wife. "Why don't we
go down to dinner, my darling? We've got a
long day ahead of us tomorrow." He ad-
justed his watch by three hours and added,
"So perhaps it would be wise to have an
early night."

Maureen placed a long silk nightdress on
her side of the bed and smiled in agreement. As she turned to place her empty
case in the wardrobe, Dick slipped an Evian
bottle from the bedside table into his jacket
pocket. He then accompanied his wife
down to the dining room.

The head waiter guided them to a quiet
table in the corner and, once they were

seated, offered his two guests menus. Maureen disappeared behind the large leather cover while she considered the table d'hôte, which allowed Dick enough time to remove the bottle of Evian from his pocket, undo the cap and fill his wife's glass.

Once they had both selected their meals, Maureen went over her proposed itinerary for the next two days. "I think we should begin with the Hermitage, first thing in the morning," she suggested, "take a break for lunch, and then spend the rest of the afternoon at the Summer Palace."

"What about the amber collection?" asked Dick, as he topped up her water glass. "I thought that was a no-miss."

"I'd already scheduled in the amber collection and the Russian Museum for Sunday."

"Sounds as if you have everything well organized," said Dick, as a waiter placed a bowl of borscht in front of his wife.

Maureen spent the rest of the meal telling Dick about some of the treasures that they would see when they visited the Hermitage. By the time Dick had signed the bill, Maureen had drunk the bottle of water.

Dick slipped the empty bottle back in his

pocket. Once they had returned to their room, he filled it with tap water and left it in the bathroom.

By the time Dick had undressed and climbed into bed, Maureen was still studying her guidebook.

"I feel exhausted," Dick said. "It must be the time change." He turned his back on her, hoping she wouldn't work out that it was just after eight p.m. in England.

Dick woke the following morning feeling very thirsty. He looked at the empty bottle of Evian on his side of the bed and remembered just in time. He climbed out of bed, walked across to the fridge and selected a bottle of orange juice.

"Will you be going to the gym this morning?" he asked a half-awake Maureen.

"Do I have time?"

"Sure, the Hermitage doesn't open until ten, and one of the reasons I always stay here is because of the hotel's gym."

"So what about you?"

"I still have to make some phone calls if everything is to be set up for Monday."

Maureen slipped out of bed and disappeared into the bathroom, which allowed

Dick enough time to top up her glass and replace the empty bottle of Evian on her side of the bed.

When Maureen emerged a few minutes later, she checked her watch before slipping on her gym kit. "I should be back in about forty minutes," she said, after tying up her trainers.

"Don't forget to take some water with you," said Dick, handing her one of the bottles from the table by the window. "They may not have one in the gym."

"Thank you," she said.

Dick wondered, from the expression on her face, if he was being just a little too solicitous.

While Maureen was in the gym, Dick took a shower. When he walked back into the bedroom, he was pleased to see that the sun was shining. He put on a blazer and slacks, but only after he'd checked that none of the bottles had been replaced by the hotel staff while he'd been in the bathroom.

Dick ordered breakfast for both of them, which arrived moments after Maureen returned from the gym, clutching the half-empty Evian bottle.

"How did your training go?" Dick asked.

"Not great," Maureen replied. "I felt a bit listless."

"Probably just jetlag," suggested Dick as he took his place on the far side of the table. He poured his wife a glass of water, and himself another orange juice. Dick opened a copy of the *Herald Tribune*, which he began to read while he waited for his wife to dress. Hillary Clinton said she wouldn't be running for president, which only convinced Dick that she would, especially as she made the announcement standing by her husband's side.

Maureen came out of the bathroom wearing a hotel dressing gown. She took the seat opposite her husband and sipped the water.

"Better take a bottle of Evian with us when we visit the Hermitage," said Maureen. Dick looked up from behind his paper. "The girl in the gym warned me not, under any circumstances, to drink the local water."

"Oh yes, I should have warned you," said Dick, as Maureen took a bottle from the table by the window and put it in her bag. "Can't be too careful."

*   *   *

Dick and Maureen strolled through the front gates of the Hermitage a few minutes before ten, to find themselves at the back of a long queue. The crocodile of visitors progressed slowly forward along an unshaded cobbled path. Maureen took several sips of water between turning the pages of the guidebook. It was ten forty before they reached the ticket booth. Once inside, Maureen continued to study her guidebook. "Whatever we do, we must be sure to see Michelangelo's *Crouching Boy*, Raphael's *Virgin*, and Leonardo's *Madonna Benois*."

Dick smiled his agreement, but knew he wouldn't be concerning himself with the masters.

As they climbed the wide marble staircase, they passed several magnificent statues nestled in alcoves. Dick was surprised to discover just how vast the Hermitage was. Despite visiting St. Petersburg several times during the past three years, he had only ever seen the building from the outside.

"Housed on three floors, Tsar Peter's collection displays treasures in over two hundred rooms," Maureen told him, reading from the guidebook. "So let's get started."

By eleven thirty they had only covered the Dutch and Italian schools on the first floor, by which time Maureen had finished the large bottle of Evian.

Dick volunteered to go and buy another bottle. He left his wife admiring Caravaggio's *The Lute Player*, while he slipped into the nearest rest room. He refilled the empty Evian bottle with tap water before rejoining his wife. If Maureen had spent a little time studying one of the many drinks counters situated on each floor, she would have discovered that the Hermitage doesn't stock Evian, because it has an exclusive contract with Volvic.

By twelve thirty they had all but covered the sixteen rooms devoted to the Renaissance artists, and agreed it was time for lunch. They left the building and strolled back into the midday sun. The two of them walked for a while along the bank of the Moika River, stopping only to take a photograph of a bride and groom posing on the Blue Bridge in front of the Mariinsky Palace.

"A local tradition," said Maureen, turning another page of her guidebook.

After walking another block, they came to a halt outside a small pizzeria. Its sensible square tables with neat red-and-white check tablecloths and smartly dressed waiters tempted them inside.

"I must go to the loo," said Maureen. "I'm feeling a little queasy. It must be the heat." She added, "Just order me a salad and a glass of water."

Dick smiled, removed the Evian bottle from her bag and filled up the glass on her side of the table. When the waiter appeared, Dick ordered a salad for his wife, and ravioli plus a large diet coke for himself. He was desperate for something to drink.

Once she'd eaten her salad, Maureen perked up a little, and even began to tell Dick what they should look out for when they visited the Summer Palace.

On the long taxi ride through the north of the city, she continued to read extracts from her guidebook. "Peter the Great built the Summer Palace after he had visited Versailles, and on returning to Russia employed the finest landscape gardeners and most gifted craftsmen in the land to reproduce the French masterpiece. He intended the finished work to be a homage to the French, whom he greatly admired as the leaders of style throughout Europe."

The taxi driver interrupted her flow with a snippet of information of his own. "We are just passing the recently constructed Winter Palace, which is where President Putin stays whenever he's in St. Petersburg." The driver paused. "And, as the national flag is flying, he must be in town."

"He's flown down from Moscow especially to see me," said Dick.

The taxi driver dutifully laughed.

The taxi drove through the gates of the Summer Palace half an hour later and the driver dropped his passengers off in a crowded carpark, bustling with sightseers and traders, who were standing behind their makeshift stalls plying their cheap souvenirs.

"Let's go and see the real thing," suggested Maureen.

"I wait for you here," said the taxi driver. "No extra charge. How long?" he added.

"I should think we'd be a couple of hours," said Dick. "No more."

"I wait for you here," he repeated.

The two of them strolled around the magnificent gardens, and Dick could see why it was described in the guidebooks as a "can't afford to miss," with five stars. Maureen continued to brief him between sips of water. "The grounds surrounding the palace cover over a hundred acres, with more than twenty fountains, as well as eleven other palatial residences." Although the sun was no longer burning down, the sky was still clear and Maureen continued to take regular gulps of water, but however many times she offered the bottle to Dick, he always replied, "No thanks."

When they finally climbed the steps of the palace, they were greeted by another long queue, and Maureen admitted that she was feeling a little tired.

"Pity to have traveled this far," said Dick, "and not take a look inside."

His wife reluctantly agreed.

When they reached the front of the queue, Dick purchased two entrance tickets and, for a small extra charge, selected an English-speaking guide to show them around.

"I don't feel too good," said Maureen as they entered the Empress Catherine's bedroom. She clung onto the four-poster bed.

"You must drink lots of water on such a hot day," suggested the tour guide helpfully. By the time they had reached Tsar Nicholas IV's study, Maureen warned her husband that she thought she was going to faint. Dick apologized to their guide, put an arm around his wife's shoulder and assisted her out of the palace on an unsteady journey back to the carpark. They found their taxi driver standing by his car waiting for them.

"We must return to the Grand Palace Hotel immediately," said Dick, as his wife fell into the back seat of the car like a drunk who has been thrown out of a pub on a Saturday night.

On the long drive back to St. Petersburg, Maureen was violently sick in the back of the taxi, but the driver didn't comment, just maintained a steady speed as he continued along the highway. Forty minutes later, he came to a halt outside the Grand Palace Hotel. Dick handed over a wodge of notes and apologized.

"Hope madam better soon," he said.

"Yes, let's hope so," replied Dick.

Dick helped his wife out of the back of the car, and guided her up the steps into the hotel lobby and quickly toward the lifts, not wishing to draw attention to himself. He had her safely back in their suite moments later. Maureen immediately disappeared into the bathroom, and even with the door closed Dick could hear her retching. He searched around the room. In their absence, all the bottles of Evian had been replaced. He only bothered to empty the one by Maureen's bedside, which he refilled with tap water from the kitchenette.

Maureen finally emerged from the bathroom, and collapsed onto the bed. "I feel awful," she said.

"Perhaps you ought to take a couple of aspirin, and try to get some sleep?"

Maureen nodded weakly. "Could you fetch them for me? They're in my wash bag."

"Of course, my darling." Once he'd found the pills, he filled a glass with tap water, before returning to his wife's side. She had taken off her dress, but not her slip. Dick helped her to sit up and became aware for the first time that she was soaked in sweat. She swilled down the two aspirins with the glass of water Dick offered her. He lowered her gently down onto the pillow before drawing the curtains. He then strolled across to the bedroom door, opened it, and placed the *Do Not Disturb* sign on the door knob. The last thing he needed was for a solicitous maid to come barging in and find his wife in her present state. Once Dick was certain she was asleep, he went down to dinner.

"Will madam be joining you this evening?" inquired the head waiter, once Dick was seated.

"No, sadly not," replied Dick, "she has a slight migraine. Too much sun I fear, but I'm sure she'll be fine by the morning."

"Let's hope so, sir. What can I interest you in tonight?"

Dick took his time perusing the menu, before he eventually said, "I think I'll start with the foie gras, followed by a rump steak—" he paused—"medium rare."

"Excellent choice, sir."

Dick poured himself a glass of water from the bottle on the table and quickly gulped it down, before filling his glass a second time. He didn't hurry his meal, and when he returned to his suite just after ten, he was delighted to find his wife was fast asleep. He picked up her glass, took it to the bathroom and refilled it with tap water. He then put it back on her side of the bed. Dick took his time undressing, before finally slipping under the covers to settle down next to his wife. He turned out the bedside light and slept soundly.

When Dick woke the following morning, he found that he too was covered in sweat. The sheets were also soaked, and when he turned over to look at his wife all the color had drained from her cheeks.

Dick eased himself out of bed, slipped

into the bathroom and took a long shower. Once he had dried himself, he put on one of the hotel's toweling dressing gowns and returned to the bedroom. He crept over to his wife's side of the bed and once again refilled her empty glass with tap water. She had clearly woken during the night, but not disturbed him.

He drew the curtains before checking that the *Do Not Disturb* sign was still on the door. He returned to his wife's side of the bed, pulled up a chair and began to read the *Herald Tribune*. He had reached the sports pages by the time she woke. Her words were slurred. She managed, "I feel awful." A long pause followed before she added, "Don't you think I ought to see a doctor?"

"He's already been to examine you, my dear," said Dick. "I called for him last night. Don't you remember? He told you that you'd caught a fever, and you'll just have to sweat it out."

"Did he leave any pills?" asked Maureen plaintively.

"No, my darling. He just said you weren't to eat anything, but to try and drink as much water as possible." He held the glass up to her lips and she attempted to gulp some more down. She even managed, "Thank you," before collapsing back onto the pillow.

"Don't worry, my darling," said Dick. "You're going to be just fine, and I promise you I won't leave your side, even for a moment." He leaned over and kissed her on the forehead. She fell asleep again.

The only time Dick left Maureen's side that day was to assure the housekeeper that his wife did not wish to have the sheets changed, to refill the glass of water on her bedside table, and late in the afternoon to take a call from the minister.

"The President flew in yesterday," were Chenkov's opening words. "He's staying at the Winter Palace, where I've just left him. He wanted me to let you know how much he is looking forward to meeting you and your wife."

"How kind of him," said Dick, "but I have a problem."

"A problem?" said a man who didn't like problems, especially when the President was in town.

"It's just that Maureen seems to have caught a fever. We were out in the sun all day yesterday, and I'm not sure that she will have fully recovered in time to join us for the signing ceremony, so I may be on my own."

"I'm sorry to hear that," said Chenkov, "and how are you?"

"Never felt better," said Dick.

"That's good," said Chenkov, sounding relieved. "So I'll pick you up at nine o'clock, as agreed. I don't want to keep the President waiting."

"Neither do I, Anatol," Dick assured him. "You'll find me standing in the lobby long before nine."

There was a knock on the door. Dick quickly put the phone down and rushed across to open it before anyone was given a chance to barge in. A maid was standing in the corridor next to a trolley laden with sheets, towels, bars of soap, shampoo bottles and cases of Evian water.

"You want the bed turned down, sir?" she asked, giving him a smile.

"No, thank you," said Dick. "My wife is not feeling well." He pointed to the *Do Not Disturb* sign.

"More water, perhaps?" she suggested, holding up a large bottle of Evian.

"No," he repeated firmly and closed the door.

The only other call that evening came from the hotel manager. He asked politely if madam would like to see the hotel doctor.

"No, thank you," said Dick. "She just caught a little sun but she's on the mend, and I feel sure she will have fully recovered by the morning."

"Just give me a call," said the manager, "should she change her mind. The doctor can be with you in minutes."

"That's very considerate of you," said Dick, "but it won't be necessary," he added before putting the phone down. He returned to his wife's side. Her skin was now pallid and blotchy. He leaned forward until he was almost touching her lips—she was still breathing. He walked across to the fridge, opened it and took out all the unopened bottles of Evian water. He placed two of them in the bathroom, and one each side of the bed. His final action, before undressing, was to take the DON'T DRINK THE WATER sign out of his suitcase and replace it on the side of the washbasin.

Chenkov's car pulled up outside the Grand Palace Hotel a few minutes before nine the following morning. Karl jumped out to open the back door for the minister.

Chenkov walked quickly up the steps and into the hotel, expecting to find Dick waiting for him in the lobby. He looked up and down the crowded corridor, but there was no sign of his business partner. He marched across to the reception desk and asked if Mr. Barnsley had left a message for him.

"No, Minister," replied the concierge. "Would you like me to call his room?" The minister nodded briskly. They both waited for some time, before the concierge added, "No one is answering the phone, Minister, so perhaps Mr. Barnsley is on his way down."

Chenkov nodded again, and began pacing up and down the lobby, continually glancing toward the elevator, before checking his watch. At ten past nine, the minister became even more anxious, as he had no desire to keep the President waiting. He returned to the reception desk.

"Try again," he demanded.

The concierge immediately dialed Mr. Barnsley's room number, but could only report that there was still no reply.

"Send for the manager," barked the minister. The concierge nodded, picked up the phone once again and dialed a single number. A few moments later, a tall, elegantly dressed man in a dark suit was standing by Chenkov's side.

"How may I assist you, Minister?" he asked.

"I need to go up to Mr. Barnsley's room."

"Of course, Minister, please follow me."

When the three men arrived on the ninth floor, they quickly made their way to the Tolstoy Suite, where they found the *Do Not Disturb* sign hanging from the door knob. The minister banged loudly on the door, but there was no response.

"Open the door," he demanded. The concierge obeyed without hesitation.

The minister marched into the room, followed by the manager and the concierge. Chenkov came to an abrupt halt when he saw two motionless bodies lying in bed. The concierge didn't need to be told to call for a doctor.

Sadly, the doctor had attended three such cases in the past month, but with a difference—they had all been locals. He studied his two patients for some time before he passed a judgment.

"The Siberian disease," he confirmed, almost in a whisper. He paused and, looking up at the minister, added, "The lady undoubtedly died during the night, whereas the gentleman has passed away within the last hour."

The minister made no comment.

"My initial conclusion," continued the doctor, "is that she probably caught the disease from drinking too much of the local water—" he paused as he looked down at Dick's lifeless body—"while her husband must have contracted the virus from his wife, probably during the night. Not an uncommon occurrence among married couples," he added. "Like so many of our countrymen, he clearly wasn't aware that—" he hesitated before uttering the word in front of the minister—"*Siberius* is one of those rare diseases that is not only infectious but highly contagious."

"But I called him last night," protested the manager, "and asked if he'd like to see a doctor, and he said it wasn't necessary, as his wife was on the mend and he was confident that she would be fully recovered by the morning."

"How sad," said the doctor, before adding, "if only he'd said yes. It would have been too late to revive his wife, but I still might have saved him."

It Can't Be
October Already

Patrick O'Flynn stood in front of H. Samuel, the jeweler's, holding a brick in his right hand. He was staring intently at the window. He smiled, raised his arm and hurled the brick at the glass pane. The window shattered like a spider's web, but remained firmly in place. An alarm was immediately set off, which in the still of a clear, cold October night could be heard half a mile away. More important to Pat, the alarm was directly connected to the local police station.

Pat didn't move as he continued to stare at his handiwork. He only had to wait ninety seconds before he heard the sound of a

siren in the distance. He bent down and retrieved the brick from the pavement, as the
whining noise grew louder and louder.
When the police car came to a screeching
halt by the curbside, Pat raised the brick
above his head and leaned back, like an
Olympic javelin thrower intent on a gold
medal. Two policemen leaped out of the car.
The older one ignored Pat, who remained
poised, arm above his head with the brick in
his hand, and walked across to the window

to check the damage. Although the pane was shattered, it was still firmly in place. In any case, an iron security grille had descended behind the window, something Pat knew full well would happen. But when the sergeant returned to the station, he would still have to phone the manager, get him out of bed and ask him to come down to the shop and turn off the alarm.

The sergeant turned round to find Pat still standing with the brick high above his head.

"OK, Pat, hand it over and get in," said the sergeant, as he held open the back door of the police car.

Pat smiled, passed the brick to the fresh-faced constable and said, "You'll need this as evidence."

The young constable was speechless.

"Thank you, Sergeant," said Pat as he climbed into the back of the car, and, smiling at the young constable, who took his place behind the wheel, asked, "Have I ever told you about the time I tried to get a job on a building site in Liverpool?"

"Many times," interjected the sergeant, as he took his place next to Pat and pulled the back door closed.

"No handcuffs?" queried Pat.

"I don't want to be handcuffed to you," said the sergeant, "I want to be rid of you. Why don't you just go back to Ireland?"

"An altogether inferior class of prison," Pat explained, "and in any case, they don't treat me with the same degree of respect as you do, Sergeant," he added, as the car moved away from the curb and headed back toward the police station.

"Can you tell me your name?" Pat asked, leaning forward to address the young constable.

"Constable Cooper."

"Are you by any chance related to Chief Inspector Cooper?"

"He's my father."

"A gentleman," said Pat. "We've had many a cup of tea and biscuits together. I hope he's in fine fettle."

"He's just retired," said Constable Cooper.

"I'm sorry to hear that," said Pat. "Will you tell him that Pat O'Flynn asked after him? And please send him, and your dear mother, my best wishes."

"Stop taking the piss, Pat," said the sergeant. "The boy's only been out of Peel House for a few weeks," he added, as the car came to a halt outside the police station. The sergeant climbed out of the back and held the door open for Pat.

"Thank you, Sergeant," said Pat, as if he was addressing the doorman at the Ritz. The constable grinned as the sergeant accompanied Pat up the stairs and into the police station.

"Ah, and a very good evening to you, Mr. Baker," said Pat when he saw who it was standing behind the desk.

"Oh, Christ," said the duty sergeant. "It can't be October already."

"I'm afraid so, Sergeant," said Pat. "I was wondering if my usual cell is available. I'll only be staying overnight, you understand."

"I'm afraid not," said the desk sergeant, "it's already occupied by a real criminal. You'll have to be satisfied with cell number two."

"But I've always had cell number one in the past," protested Pat.

The desk sergeant looked up and raised an eyebrow.

"No, I'm to blame," admitted Pat, "I should have asked my secretary to call and book in advance. Do you need to take an imprint of my credit card?"

"No, I have all your details on file," the desk sergeant assured him.

"How about fingerprints?"

"Unless you've found a way of removing your old ones, Pat, I don't think we need another set. But I suppose you'd better sign the charge sheet."

Pat took the proffered biro and signed on the bottom line with a flourish.

"Take him down to cell number two, Constable."

"Thank you, Sergeant," said Pat as he was led away. He stopped, turned around and said, "I wonder, Sergeant, if you could give me a wake-up call around seven, a cup of tea, Earl Gray preferably, and a copy of the *Irish Times*."

"Piss off, Pat," said the desk sergeant, as the constable tried to stifle a laugh.

"Which reminds me," said Pat, "have I told you about the time I tried to get a job on a building site in Liverpool, and the foreman—"

"Get him out of my sight, Constable, if you don't want to spend the rest of the month on traffic duty."

The constable grabbed Pat by the elbow and hurried him downstairs.

"No need to come with me," said Pat. "I can find my own way." This time the constable did laugh as he placed a key in the lock of cell number two. The young policeman unlocked the cell and pulled open the heavy door, allowing Pat to stroll in.

"Thank you, Constable Cooper," said Pat. "I look forward to seeing you in the morning."

"I'll be off duty," said Constable Cooper.

"Then I'll see you this time next year," said Pat without explanation, "and don't forget to pass on my best wishes to your father," he added as the four-inch-thick iron door was slammed shut.

Pat studied the cell for a few moments: a steel washbasin, a bog and a bed, one sheet, one blanket and one pillow. Pat was reassured by the fact that nothing had changed since last year. He fell on the horsehair mattress, placed his head on the rock-hard pillow and slept all night—for the first time in weeks.

Pat was woken from a deep sleep at seven the following morning, when the cell-door flap was flicked open and two black eyes stared in.

"Good morning, Pat," said a friendly voice.

"Good morning, Wesley," said Pat, not even opening his eyes. "And how are you?"

"I'm well," replied Wesley, "but sorry to see you back." He paused. "I suppose it must be October."

"It certainly is," said Pat climbing off the bed, "and it's important that I look my best for this morning's show trial."

"Anything you need in particular?"

"A cup of tea would be most acceptable, but what I really require is a razor, a bar of soap, a toothbrush and some toothpaste. I don't have to remind you, Wesley, that a defendant is entitled to this simple request before he makes an appearance in court."

"I'll see you get them," said Wesley, "and would you like to read my copy of the *Sun*?"

"That's kind of you, Wesley, but if the chief superintendent has finished with yesterday's *Times*, I'd prefer that." A West Indian chuckle was followed by the closing of the shutter on the cell door.

Pat didn't have to wait long before he heard a key turn in the lock. The heavy door was pulled open to reveal the smiling face of Wesley Pickett, a tray in one hand, which he placed on the end of the bed.

"Thank you, Wesley," said Pat as he stared down at the bowl of cornflakes, small carton of skimmed milk, two slices of burned toast and a boiled egg. "I do hope Molly remembered," added Pat, "that I like my eggs lightly boiled, for two and a half minutes."

"Molly left last year," said Wesley. "I think you'll find the egg was boiled last night by the desk sergeant."

"You can't get the staff nowadays," said Pat. "I blame it on the Irish, myself. They're no longer committed to domestic service," he added as he tapped the top of his egg with a plastic spoon. "Wesley, have I told you about the time I tried to get a laboring job on a building site in Liverpool, and the foreman, a bloody Englishman—" Pat looked up and sighed as he heard the door slam and the key turn in the lock. "I suppose I must have told him the story before," he muttered to himself.

After Pat had finished breakfast, he cleaned his teeth with a toothbrush and a tube of toothpaste that were even smaller than the ones they'd supplied on his only experience of an Aer Lingus flight to Dublin. Next, he turned on the hot tap in the tiny steel washbasin. The slow trickle of water took some time to turn from cold to luke-warm. He rubbed the mean piece of soap between his fingers until he'd whipped up enough cream to produce a lather, which he then smeared all over his stubbled face. Next he picked up the plastic Bic razor, and began the slow process of removing a four-day-old stubble. He finally dabbed his face with a rough green hand towel, not much larger than a flannel.

Pat sat on the end of the bed and, while he waited, read Wesley's *Sun* from cover to cover in four minutes. Only an article by their political editor Trevor Kavanagh—he must surely be an Irishman, thought Pat—was worthy of his attention. Pat's thoughts were interrupted when the heavy metal door was pulled open once again.

"Let's be 'avin you, Pat," said Sergeant Webster. "You're first on this morning."

Pat accompanied the officer back up the stairs, and when he saw the desk sergeant, asked, "Could I have my valuables back, Mr. Baker? You'll find them in the safe."

"Like what?" said the desk sergeant, looking up.

"My pearl cufflinks, the Cartier Tank watch and a silver-topped cane engraved with my family crest."

"I flogged 'em all off last night, Pat," said the desk sergeant.

"Probably for the best," remarked Pat. "I won't be needing them where I'm going," he added, before following Sergeant Webster out of the front door and onto the pavement.

"Jump in the front," said the sergeant, as he climbed behind the wheel of a panda car.

"But I'm entitled to two officers to escort me to court," insisted Pat. "It's a Home Office regulation."

"It may well be a Home Office regulation," the sergeant replied, "but we're short-staffed this morning, two off sick, and one away on a training course."

"But what if I tried to escape?"

"A blessed release," said Sergeant Webster, as he pulled away from the curb, "because that would save us all a lot of trouble."

"And what would you do if I decided to punch you?"

"I'd punch you back," said an exasperated sergeant.

"That's not very friendly," suggested Pat.

"Sorry, Pat," said the sergeant. "It's just that I promised my wife that I'd be off duty by ten this morning, so we could go shopping." He paused. "So she won't be best pleased with me—or you for that matter."

"I apologize, Sergeant Webster," said Pat. "Next October I'll try to find out which shift you're on, so I can be sure to avoid it. Perhaps you'd pass on my apologies to Mrs. Webster."

The sergeant would have laughed, if it had been anyone else, but he knew Pat meant it.

"Any idea who I'll be up in front of this morning?" asked Pat as the car came to a halt at a set of traffic lights.

"Thursday," said the sergeant, as the lights turned green and he pushed the gear lever back into first. "It must be Perkins."

"Councillor Arnold Perkins OBE, oh good," said Pat. "He's got a very short fuse. So if he doesn't give me a long enough sentence, I'll just have to light it," he added as the car swung into the private carpark at the back of Marylebone Road Magistrates'

Court. A court officer was heading toward the police car just as Pat stepped out.

"Good morning, Mr. Adams," said Pat.

"When I looked at the list of defendants this morning, Pat, and saw your name," said Mr. Adams, "I assumed it must be that time of the year when you make your annual appearance. Follow me, Pat, and let's get this over with as quickly as possible."

Pat accompanied Mr. Adams through the back door of the courthouse and on down the long corridor to a holding cell.

"Thank you, Mr. Adams," said Pat as he took a seat on a thin wooden bench that was cemented to a wall along one side of the large oblong room. "If you'd be kind enough to just leave me for a few moments," Pat added, "so that I can compose myself before the curtain goes up."

Mr. Adams smiled, and turned to leave.

"By the way," said Pat, as Mr. Adams touched the handle of the door, "did I tell you about the time I tried to get a laboring job on a building site in Liverpool, but the foreman, a bloody Englishman, had the nerve to ask me—"

"Sorry, Pat, some of us have got a job to

do, and in any case, you told me that story last October." He paused. "And, come to think of it, the October before."

Pat sat silently on the bench and, as he had nothing else to read, considered the graffiti on the wall. *Perkins is a prat*. He felt able to agree with that sentiment. *Man U are the champions*. Someone had crossed out *Man U* and replaced it with *Chelsea*. Pat wondered if he should cross out Chelsea, and write in Cork, whom neither team had ever defeated. As there was no clock on the wall, Pat couldn't be sure how much time had passed before Mr. Adams finally returned to escort him up to the courtroom. Adams was now dressed in a long black gown, looking like Pat's old headmaster.

"Follow me," Mr. Adams intoned solemnly.

Pat remained unusually silent as they proceeded down the yellow brick road, as the old lags call the last few yards before you climb the steps and enter the back door of the court. Pat ended up standing in the dock, with a bailiff by his side.

Pat stared up at the bench and looked at the three magistrates who made up this

morning's panel. Something was wrong. He had been expecting to see Mr. Perkins, who had been bald this time last year, almost Pickwickian. Now, suddenly, he seemed to have sprouted a head of fair hair. On his right was Councillor Steadman, a liberal, who was much too lenient for Pat's liking. On the chairman's left sat a middle-aged lady whom Pat had never seen before; her thin lips and piggy eyes gave Pat a little confidence that the liberal could be out-voted two to one, especially if he played his cards right. Miss Piggy looked as if she would have happily supported capital punishment for shoplifters.

Sergeant Webster stepped into the witness box and took the oath.

"What can you tell us about this case, Sergeant?" Mr. Perkins asked, once the oath had been administered.

"May I refer to my notes, your honor?" asked Sergeant Webster, turning to face the chairman of the panel. Mr. Perkins nodded, and the sergeant turned over the cover of his notepad.

"I apprehended the defendant at two o'clock this morning, after he had thrown a brick at the window of H. Samuel, the jeweler's, on Mason Street."

"Did you see him throw the brick, Sergeant?"

"No, I did not," admitted Webster, "but he was standing on the pavement with the brick in his hand when I apprehended him."

"And had he managed to gain entry?" asked Perkins.

"No, sir," said the sergeant, "but he was

about to throw the brick again when I arrested him."

"The same brick?"

"I think so."

"And had he done any damage?"

"He had shattered the glass, but a security grille prevented him from removing anything."

"How valuable were the goods in the window?" asked Mr. Perkins.

"There were no goods in the window," replied the sergeant, "because the manager always locks them up in the safe, before going home at night."

Mr. Perkins looked puzzled and, glancing down at the charge sheet, said, "I see you have charged O'Flynn with attempting to break and enter."

"That is correct, sir," said Sergeant Webster, returning his notebook to a back pocket of his trousers.

Mr. Perkins turned his attention to Pat. "I note that you have entered a plea of guilty on the charge sheet, O'Flynn."

"Yes, m'lord."

"Then I'll have to sentence you to three months, unless you can offer some expla-

nation." He paused and looked down at Pat over the top of his half-moon spectacles. "Do you wish to make a statement?" he asked.

"Three months is not enough, m'lord."

"I am not a lord," said Mr. Perkins firmly.

"Oh, aren't you?" said Pat. "It's just that I thought as you were wearing a wig, which you didn't have this time last year, you must be a lord."

"Watch your tongue," said Mr. Perkins, "or I may have to consider putting your sentence up to six months."

"That's more like it, m'lord," said Pat.

"If that's more like it," said Mr. Perkins, barely able to control his temper, "then I sentence you to six months. Take the prisoner down."

"Thank you, m'lord," said Pat, and added under his breath, "see you this time next year."

The bailiff hustled Pat out of the dock and quickly down the stairs to the basement.

"Nice one, Pat," he said before locking him back up in a holding cell.

Pat remained in the holding cell while he

waited for all the necessary forms to be filled in. Several hours passed before the cell door was finally opened and he was escorted out of the courthouse to his waiting transport; not on this occasion a panda car driven by Sergeant Webster, but a long blue-and-white van with a dozen tiny cubicles inside, known as the sweat box.

"Where are they taking me this time?" Pat asked a not very communicative officer whom he'd never seen before.

"You'll find out when you get there, Paddy," was all he got in reply.

"Have I ever told you about the time I tried to get a job on a building site in Liverpool?"

"No," replied the officer, "and I don't want to 'ear—"

"—and the foreman, a bloody Englishman, had the nerve to ask me if I knew the difference between a—" Pat was shoved up the steps of the van and pushed into a little cubicle that resembled a lavatory on a plane. He fell onto the plastic seat as the door was slammed behind him.

Pat stared out of the tiny square window,
and when the vehicle turned south onto
Baker Street, realized it had to be Belmarsh.
Pat sighed. At least they've got a half-
decent library, he thought, and I may even
be able to get back my old job in the kitchen.
    When the Black Maria pulled up outside
the prison gates, his guess was confirmed.
A large green board attached to the prison

gate announced BELMARSH, and some wag had replaced BEL with HELL. The van proceeded through one set of double-barred gates, and then another, before finally coming to a halt in a barren yard.

Twelve prisoners were herded out of the van and marched up the steps to an induction area, where they waited in line. Pat smiled when he reached the front of the queue and saw who was behind the desk, checking them all in.

"And how are we this fine pleasant evening, Mr. Jenkins?" Pat asked.

The Senior Officer looked up from behind his desk and said, "It can't be October already."

"It most certainly is, Mr. Jenkins," Pat confirmed, "and may I offer my commiserations on your recent loss."

"My recent loss," repeated Mr. Jenkins. "What are you talking about, Pat?"

"Those fifteen Welshmen who appeared in Dublin earlier this year, passing themselves off as a rugby team."

"Don't push your luck, Pat."

"Would I, Mr. Jenkins, when I was hoping that you would allocate me my old cell?"

The SO ran his finger down the list of

available cells. "'Fraid not, Pat," he said with an exaggerated sigh, "it's already double-booked. But I've got just the person for you to spend your first night with," he added, before turning to the night officer. "Why don't you escort O'Flynn to cell one nineteen."

The night officer looked uncertain, but after a further look from Mr. Jenkins, all he said was, "Follow me, Pat."

"So who has Mr. Jenkins selected to be my pad mate on this occasion?" inquired Pat, as the night officer accompanied him down the long, gray-brick corridor before coming to a halt at the first set of double-barred gates. "Is it to be Jack the Ripper, or Michael Jackson?"

"You'll find out soon enough," responded the night officer as the second of the barred gates slid open.

"Have I ever told you," asked Pat, as they walked out on to the ground floor of B block, "about the time I tried to get a job on a building site in Liverpool, and the foreman, a bloody Englishman, had the nerve to ask me if I knew the difference between a joist and a girder?"

Pat waited for the officer to respond, as

they came to a halt outside cell number 119. He placed a large key in the lock.

"No, Pat, you haven't," the night officer said as he pulled open the heavy door. "So what is the difference between a joist and a girder?" he demanded.

Pat was about to reply, but when he looked into the cell was momentarily silenced.

"Good evening, m'lord," said Pat, for the second time that day. The night officer didn't wait for a reply. He slammed the door closed, and turned the key in the lock.

Pat spent the rest of the evening telling me, in graphic detail, all that had taken place since two o'clock that morning. When he had finally come to the end of his tale, I simply asked, "Why October?"

"Once the clocks go back," said Pat, "I prefer to be inside, where I'm guaranteed three meals a day and a cell with central heating. Sleeping rough is all very well in the summer, but it's not so clever during an English winter."

"But what would you have done if Mr. Perkins had sentenced you to a year?" I asked.

"I'd have been on my best behavior from day one," said Pat, "and they would have released me in six months. They have a real problem with overcrowding at the moment," he explained.

"But if Mr. Perkins had stuck to his original sentence of just three months, you would have been released in January, midwinter."

"Not a hope," said Pat. "Just before I was due to be let out, I would have been found with a bottle of Guinness in my cell. A misdemeanor for which the governor is obliged to automatically add a further three months to your sentence, and that would have taken me comfortably through to April."

I laughed. "And is that how you intend to spend the rest of your life?" I asked.

"I don't think that far ahead," admitted Pat. "Six months is quite enough to be going on with," he added, as he climbed on to the top bunk and switched off the light.

"Goodnight, Pat," I said, as I rested my head on the pillow.

"Have I ever told you about the time I tried to get a job on a building site in Liverpool?" asked Pat, just as I was falling asleep.

"No, you haven't," I replied.

"Well, the foreman, a bloody Englishman, no offense intended—" I smiled—"had the nerve to ask me if I knew the difference between a joist and a girder."

"And do you?" I asked.

"I most certainly do. Joyce wrote *Ulysses*, and Goethe wrote *Faust*."

Patrick O'Flynn died of hypothermia on 23 November 2005, while sleeping under the arches on Victoria Embankment in central London.

His body was discovered by a young constable, just a hundred yards away from the Savoy Hotel.

The Red King

"They charged me with the wrong offense, and sentenced me for the wrong crime," Max said as he lay in the bunk below me, rolling another cigarette.

While I was in prison, I heard this claim voiced by inmates on several occasions, but in the case of Max Glover it turned out to be true.

Max was serving a three-year sentence for obtaining money by false pretenses. Not his game. Max's speciality was removing small items from large homes. He once told me, with considerable professional pride, that it could be years before an owner became aware that a family heirloom has gone missing, especially, Max added, if you take one small, but valuable, object from a cluttered room.

"Mind you," continued Max, "I'm not complaining, because if they had charged me with the crime I did commit, I would have ended up with a much longer sentence—" he paused—"and nothing to look forward to once I'm released."

Max knew he had aroused my curiosity, and as I had nowhere to go for the next three hours before the cell door would be opened for Association—that glorious forty-five minutes when prisoners are allowed out of their cell for a stroll around the yard—I picked up my pen, and said, "OK, Max, I'm hooked. So tell me how you came to be sentenced for the wrong crime."

Max struck a match, lit his hand-rolled cigarette and inhaled deeply before he began. In prison, every action is exaggerated, as no one is in a hurry. I lay on the bunk above and waited patiently.

"Does the Kennington Set mean anything to you?" Max began.

"No," I replied, assuming he must be referring to a group of red-coated gentlemen on horseback, glass of port in one hand, whip in the other, surrounded by a pack of hounds with intent to spend their Saturday morning in pursuit of a furry animal with a bushy tail. I was wrong. The Kennington Set, as Max went on to explain, was in fact a chess set.

"But no ordinary chess set," he assured me. I became more interested. The pieces were probably crafted by Lu Ping (1469–1540), a master craftsman of the Ming Dynasty (1368–1644). All thirty-two ivory pieces were exquisitely carved and then delicately painted in red and white. The details have been faithfully recorded in several historic documents, though it has never been conclusively established exactly how many sets Lu Ping was responsible for producing in his lifetime.

"Three complete sets were known to be in existence," continued Max as smoke spiraled up from the lower bunk. "The first is displayed in the throne room of the People's Palace in Peking; the second in the Mellon Collection in Washington, and the third at the British Museum. Many collectors scoured the great continent of China in search of the fabled fourth set, and although such efforts always ended in failure, several individual pieces appeared on the market from time to time."

Max stubbed out the smallest cigarette butt I have ever seen. "I was at the time," continued Max, "carrying out some research into the smaller objects of Kennington Hall in Yorkshire."

"How did you manage that?" I asked.

"*Country Life* commissioned Lord Kennington to write a coffee table book for Christmas, in which he detailed the treasures of Kennington Hall," Max said, before rolling a second cigarette. "Most considerate of him," he added.

"Among the peer's ancestors was one James Kennington (1552–1618), a true adventurer, buccaneer, and loyal servant of Queen Elizabeth I. James rescued the first set in 1588, only moments before he sunk the *Isabella*. On returning to Plymouth, following a seventeen–four victory in the match against the Spanish, Captain Kennington lavished treasure plundered from the sinking ship on his monarch. Her Majesty always showed a great deal of interest in anything solid, especially if she could wear it—gold, silver, pearls or rare gems—and rewarded Captain Kennington with a knighthood. Elizabeth had no use for the chess set, so Sir James was stuck with it. Unlike Sir Francis or Sir Walter, Sir James continued to plunder the high seas. He was so successful that, a decade later, his monarch elevated him to the House of Lords, with the title the first Lord Kennington, for services rendered to the Crown." Max paused before adding, "The only difference between a pirate and a peer is who you divide the spoils with."

The second Lord Kennington, like his monarch, showed no interest in chess, so the set was left to gather dust in one of the ninety-two rooms in Kennington Hall. As there were few historical incidents worthy of mention during the uneventful lives of the third, fourth, fifth or sixth Lords Kennington, we can only assume that the remarkable chess set remained in situ, its pieces never moved in anger. The seventh Lord Kennington served as a colonel in the 12th Light Dragoons at the time of Waterloo. The colonel played the occasional game of chess, so the set was dusted down and returned to the Long Gallery.

The eighth Lord Kennington was slaughtered during the Charge of the Light Brigade, the ninth in the Boer War, and the tenth at Ypres. The eleventh, a playboy, led a more peaceful life, but eventually found it necessary, for pecuniary reasons— Kennington Hall required a new roof—to open his home to the public. They turned up every weekend in countless numbers, and for a small sum were allowed to stroll around the Hall; when they ventured into the Long Gallery they came across the Chinese masterpiece on its stand, surrounded by a red rope.

With mounting debts, which the public's entrance fees could not offset, the eleventh Lord Kennington was forced to sell off several of the family heirlooms, including the Kennington Set.

Christie's placed an estimate of £100,000 on the masterpiece, but the auctioneer's hammer finally fell at £230,000.

"When you next visit Washington," added Max between puffs, "you can view the original Kennington Set, as it's now part of the Mellon Collection. This would have been the end of my tale," continued Max, "if the eleventh Lord Kennington hadn't married an American striptease artiste, who gave birth to a son. This child displayed a quality that the Kennington lineage had not troubled themselves with for several generations—brains.

"The Honorable Harry Kennington became, much to the disapproval of his father, a hedge-fund manager, and thus the natural heir to the first Lord Kennington. He was a man who took as easily to the currency market as his pirate ancestor had to the high seas. By the age of twenty-seven, Harry had plundered his first million as an asset stripper, much to his mother's amusement, who suggested that stripping was clearly a hereditary trait. By the time Harry inherited the title he was chairman of Kennington's Bank. The first thing he did with his new-found wealth was to set about restoring Kennington Hall to its former glory. He certainly did not allow members of the public to pay five pounds to park their cars on his front lawn.

"The twelfth Lord Kennington, like his father, also married a remarkable woman. Elsie Trumpshaw was the offspring of a Yorkshire cotton mill proprietor, and the product of a Cheltenham Ladies' College education. Like any self-respecting Yorkshire lass, Elsie considered the saying, *If you take care of the pennies, the pounds will take care of themselves* to be a creed, not a cliché.

"While her husband was away making money, Elsie was unquestionably the mistress of Kennington Hall. Having spent her formative years wearing her elder sister's hand-me-downs, carrying her thumbed books to school and later borrowing her lipstick, whatever the color, Elsie was well qualified to be the guardian of a hereditary pile. With consummate skill, diligence and good housekeeping, she set about the maintenance and upkeep of the newly restored Hall. Although she had no interest in the game of chess, she was irritated by the empty display cabinet in the Long Gallery. She finally solved the problem while strolling around a local car-boot sale," said Max, "and at the same time changed the fortunes of so many people, myself included." Max stubbed out his second cigarette and I was relieved that he didn't immediately roll another, as our little cell was fast coming to resemble Paddington Station in the era of the steam engine.

*   *   *

Elsie was trudging around a car-boot sale in Pudsey on a rainy Sunday morning—she only ever attended such events when it was raining, as that ensured fewer customers and it was therefore easier for her to strike a bargain. She was rummaging through some clothes when she came across the chess-board. The red and white squares brought back memories of a photograph she had seen in the old Christie's catalog, dating from when the original set had been sold. Elsie bargained for some time with the man standing at the back of an ancient Jaguar, and ended up having to part with £23 for the ivory chessboard.

When Elsie returned to the Hall, she placed the newly acquired board in the empty display cabinet and was delighted to discover that it was a perfect fit. She thought nothing more of the coincidence, until her uncle Bertie advised her to have it valued—for insurance purposes, he explained.

Unconvinced, but unwilling to slight her uncle, Elsie took the board up to London on one of her monthly trips to visit her aunt Gertrude. Lady Kennington—she was always Lady Kennington in London—

dropped into Sotheby's on her way to Fort-
num & Mason. A young assistant in the Chinese department asked if her ladyship
would be kind enough to come back later
that afternoon, by which time their expert
would have placed a value on the board.

Elsie returned to Sotheby's after a
leisurely lunch with Aunt Gertrude. She was
greeted by a Mr. Sencill, the head of the
Chinese department, who offered the opinion that the piece was unquestionably Ming
Dynasty.

"And are you able to place a value on it—"
she paused—"for insurance purposes?"

"Two thousand, two thousand five hundred, m'lady," said Mr. Sencill. "Ming chess-
boards are fairly common," he explained. "It
is the individual pieces that are rare, and a
complete set . . ." He raised the palms of
his hands and placed them together, as if
praying to the unseen God of auctioneers.
"Are you perhaps considering selling the
board?" he inquired.

"No," replied Elsie firmly. "On the contrary, I'm thinking of adding to it."

The expert smiled. After all, Sotheby's is
nothing more than a glorified pawn shop,

with each generation of the aristocracy either buying or selling.

On arriving back at Kennington Hall, Elsie returned the board to its position of honor in the drawing room.

Aunt Gertrude set the ball rolling. On Christmas Day she presented her niece with a white pawn. Elsie placed the single piece on the empty board. It looked lonely.

"And now, my dear, you must see if you can complete the set in your lifetime," the old lady challenged, unaware of the chain of events she was about to set in motion. What had begun as a whim, while attending a car-boot sale in Pudsey, turned into an obsession, as Elsie began to search the globe for the missing pieces. The first Lord Kennington would have been proud of her.

When Lady Kennington gave birth to their first son, Edward, a grateful husband presented his wife with a white queen. A magnificently sculptured ivory lady adorned in a long, intricately carved royal gown. Her Majesty stared down with disdain on the single pawn.

The next acquisition was another white pawn, acquired by Uncle Bertie from a dealer in New York. This allowed the white queen to reign over two of her subjects.

The birth of a second son, James, was rewarded with a red bishop, resplendent in a flowing surplice and carrying a shepherd's crook. The queen and her two subjects were now able to celebrate Holy Communion, even if they had to travel to the other side of the board to do so. Soon the whole family began to join in the search for the missing pieces. A red pawn was the next acquisition, when it came under the auctioneer's hammer at Bonham's. He took up his place on the far side of the board, waiting to be taken. By now, everyone in the trade was only too aware of Lady Kennington's lifetime mission.

Next to find its place on the board was a white castle, which Aunt Gertrude left Elsie in her will.

In 1991 the twelfth Lord Kennington passed away, by which time the white set was only lacking two pawns and a knight, while the red set was short of four pawns, one rook and a king.

On 11 May 1992, a dealer in possession of three red pawns and a white knight

knocked on the door of Kennington Hall. He had recently returned from a journey through the outer regions of China. A long and arduous trek, he told her ladyship. But, he assured her, he had not returned empty-handed.

Although her ladyship was in her declining years, she still held out for several days, before the dealer finally settled his bill at the Kennington Arms and left clutching a check for £26,000.

Despite following up rumors from Hong Kong, flying to Boston, contacting dealers as far afield as Moscow and Mexico, rumor rarely became reality in Lady Kennington's unremitting search for the last of the missing pieces.

During the next few years, Edward, the thirteenth Lord Kennington, came across the last red pawn and a red rook in the home of a penniless peer, who had been on the same staircase as Eddie at Eton. His brother James, not to be outdone, acquired two white pawns from a dealer in Bangkok.

This left only the red king to be unearthed.

The family had for some time been paying well over the odds for any missing pieces, since every dealer across the globe was well aware that if Lady Kennington was able to complete the set it would be worth a fortune.

When Elsie entered her ninth decade, she informed her sons that on her demise she planned to divide the estate equally between the two of them, with one proviso. She intended to bequeath the chess set to whichever one of them found the missing red king.

Elsie died at the age of eighty-three, without her king.

Edward had already acquired the title— something you can't dispose of in a will— and now, after death duties, also inherited the Hall and a further £857,000. James moved into the Cadogan Square apartment, and also received the sum of £857,000. The Kennington Set remained in its display case for all to admire, one square still unoccupied, ownership unresolved. Enter Max Glover.

Max had one undisputed gift, his ability to wield a willow. Educated at one of England's minor public schools, his talent as a stylish left-handed batsman allowed him to mix with the very people that he would later rob. After all, a chap who can score an effortless half century is obviously somebody one can trust.

Away fixtures suited Max best, as they allowed him the opportunity to meet eleven potential new victims. Kennington Village XI was no exception. By the time his lordship had joined the two teams for tea in the pavilion, Max had wormed out of the local umpire the history of the Kennington Set, including the provision in the will that whichever son came up with the missing red king would automatically inherit the complete set.

Max boldly asked his lordship, while devouring a portion of Victoria sponge, if he might be allowed to view the Kennington Set, as he was fascinated by the game of chess. Lord Kennington was only too happy to invite a man with such an effortless cover drive into his drawing room. The moment Max spotted the empty square, a plan began to form in his mind. A few well-planted questions were indiscreetly answered by his host. Max avoided making any reference to his lordship's brother, or the clause in the will. He then spent the rest of the afternoon at square leg, refining his plan. He dropped two catches.

When the match was over, Max declined an invitation to join the rest of the team at the village pub, explaining that he had urgent business in London.

Moments after arriving back at his flat in Hammersmith, Max phoned an old lag he'd shared a pad with when he'd been locked up in a previous establishment. The former inmate assured Max that he could deliver, but it would take him about a month and "would cost 'im."

Max chose a Sunday afternoon to return to Kennington Hall and continue his research. He left his ancient MG—soon to be-

come a collector's item, he tried to convince
himself—in the visitors' carpark. He followed
signs to the front door, where he handed
over five pounds in exchange for an entrance
ticket. Maintenance and running costs had
once again made it necessary for the Hall to
be opened to the public at weekends.

Max walked purposefully down a long
corridor adorned with ancestral portraits
painted by such luminaries as Romney,
Gainsborough, Lely and Stubbs. Each
would have fetched a fortune on the open
market, but Max's eyes were set on a far
smaller object, currently residing in the
Long Gallery.

When Max entered the room that displayed the Kennington Set, he found the
masterpiece surrounded by an attentive
group of visitors who were being addressed
by a tour guide. Max stood at the back of
the crowd and listened to a tale he knew
only too well. He waited patiently for the
group to move on to the dining room and
admire the family silver.

"Several pieces were captured at the
time of the Armada," the tour guide intoned
as the group followed him into an adjoining
room.

Max looked back down the corridor to check that the next group was not about to descend upon him. He placed a hand in his pocket and withdrew the red king. Other than the color, the intricately carved piece was identical in every detail to the white king standing on the opposite side of the board. Max knew the counterfeit would not pass a carbon-dating test, but he was satisfied that he was in possession of a perfect copy. He left Kennington Hall a few minutes later, and drove back to London.

Max's next problem was to decide which city would have the most relaxed security to carry out his coup: London, Washington or Peking. The People's Palace in Peking won by a short head. However, when it came to considering the cost of the whole exercise, the British Museum was the only horse left in the race. But what finally tipped the balance for Max was the thought of spending the next five years locked up in a Chinese jail, an American penitentiary, or residing at an open prison in the east of England. England won in a canter.

The following morning Max visited the British Museum for the first time in his life. The lady seated behind the information desk directed him to the back of the ground floor, where the Chinese collection is housed.

Max discovered that hundreds of Chinese artifacts occupied the fifteen rooms, and it took him the best part of an hour to locate the chess set. He had considered seeking guidance from one of the uniformed guards, but as he had no desire to draw attention to himself, and also doubted that they would be able to answer his question, he thought better of it.

Max had to hang around for some time before he was left alone in the room. He could not afford a member of the public or, worse, a guard, to witness his little subterfuge. Max noted that the security guard covered four rooms every thirty minutes. He would therefore have to wait until the guard had departed for the Islam room, while at the same time being sure that no other visitors were in sight, before he could make his move.

It was another hour before Max felt confident enough to take the bastard out of his pocket and compare the piece with the legitimate king, standing proudly on its red square in the display cabinet. The two kings stared at each other, identical twins, except that one was an impostor. Max glanced around—the room was still empty. After all, it was eleven o'clock on a Tuesday morning, half term, and the sun was shining.

Max waited until the guard had moved on to Islamic artifacts before he carried out his well-rehearsed move. With the help of a Swiss Army knife, he carefully prised open the lid of the display cabinet that covered the Chinese masterpiece. A raucous alarm immediately sounded, but long before the first guard appeared, Max had switched the two kings, replaced the cover of the case, opened a window and strolled casually into the next room. He was studying the costume of a samurai when two guards rushed into the adjoining room. One cursed when he spotted the open window, while the other checked to see if anything was missing.

"Now, you'll want to know," suggested Max, clearly enjoying himself, "how I trapped both brothers into a fool's mate." I nodded, but he didn't speak again until he'd rolled another cigarette. "To start with," continued Max, "never rush a transaction when you're in possession of something *two* buyers want, and in this case, *desperately* want. My next visit—" he paused to light his cigarette—"was to a shop in the Charing Cross Road. This had not required a great deal of research, because they advertised themselves in the *Yellow Pages* under Chess, as Marlowe's, *the people who serve the masters and advise the beginners*."

Max stepped into the musty old shop, to be greeted by an elderly gentleman who resembled one of life's pawns: someone who took the occasional move forward, but still looked as if he must eventually be taken— certainly not the type who reached the other side of the board to become a king. Max asked the old man about a chess set that he had spotted in the window. There then followed a series of well-rehearsed questions, which casually led to the value of a red king in the Kennington Set.

"Were such a piece ever to come onto the market," the elderly assistant mused, "the price could be in excess of fifty thousand pounds, as everyone knows there are two certain bidders."

It was this piece of information that

caused Max to make a few adjustments to his plan. His next problem was that he knew his bank account wouldn't stretch to a visit to New York. He ended up having to "acquire" several small objects from large houses, which could be disposed of quickly, so he could visit the States with enough capital to put his plan into effect. Luckily it was in the middle of the cricket season.

When Max landed at JFK, he didn't bother to visit Sotheby's or Christie's, but instead instructed the yellow cab to drive him to Phillips Auctioneers on East 79th Street. He was relieved to find that, when he produced the delicate carving stolen from the British Museum, the young assistant didn't show a great deal of interest in the piece.

"Are you aware of its provenance?" asked the assistant.

"No," replied Max, "it's been in my family for years."

Six weeks later a sales catalog was published. Max was delighted to find that Lot 23 was listed as being of no known provenance, with a high value of $300. As it was not one of the items graced with a photograph, Max felt confident that few, if any, would take much interest in the red king, and it would therefore be unlikely to come to the attention of either Edward or James Kennington. That is, until he made them aware of it.

A week before the sale was due to take place, Max rang Phillips in New York. He had only one question for the young assistant, who replied that although the catalog had been available for over a month, no one had shown any particular interest in his red king. Max feigned disappointment.

The next call Max made was to Kennington Hall. He tempted his lordship with several ifs, buts and even a maybe, which elicited an invitation to join Lord Kennington for lunch at White's.

Lord Kennington explained to his guest over a bowl of brown Windsor soup that Max could not produce any papers over lunch as it was against the club rules. Max nodded, placed the Phillips catalog under his chair, and began an elaborate tale of how by sheer accident, while viewing the figure of a mandarin on behalf of a client, he had come across the red king.

"I would have missed it myself," said

Max, "if you hadn't acquainted me with its history."

Lord Kennington did not bother with pudding (bread and butter), cheese (Cheddar) or biscuits (water), but suggested they took coffee in the library, where you are allowed to discuss business.

Max opened the Phillips catalog to reveal Lot 23, along with several loose photographs he had not shown the auctioneer. When Lord Kennington saw the estimate of three hundred dollars, his next question was, "Do you think Phillips might have told my brother about the sale?"

"There is no reason to believe so," replied Max. "I've been assured by one of the assistants working on the sale that the public have shown little interest in lot twenty-three."

"But how can you be so sure of its provenance?"

"That's what I do for a living," said Max with confidence. "But you can always have the piece carbon-dated, and if I'm proved wrong, you won't have to pay for it."

"Can't ask for more than that," said Lord Kennington, "so I suppose I'll have to fly to America and bid for the piece myself," he added, thumping the arm of the leather chair. A cloud of elderly dust rose into the air.

"I wonder if that would be wise, my lord," said Max, "after all—"

"And why not?" demanded Kennington.

"It's just that, if you were to fly to the States without explanation, it might arouse unnecessary curiosity among certain members of your family," Max paused, "and if you were then spotted in an auction house . . ."

"I take your point," said Kennington, and looking across at Max added, "so what do you advise, old boy?"

"I would be only too happy to represent your lordship's interests," said Max.

"And what would you charge for such a service?" Lord Kennington inquired.

"One thousand pounds plus expenses," said Max, "against two and a half percent of the hammer price, which I can assure you is standard practice."

Lord Kennington removed his checkbook from an inside pocket and wrote out the figure £1,000. "How much do you estimate the piece might fetch?" he asked casually.

Max was pleased that Lord Kennington

had raised the subject of price, as it would have been his next question. "That will depend on whether anyone else is privy to our little secret," said Max. "However, I would suggest that you place an upper limit of fifty thousand dollars on the piece."

"Fifty thousand?" spluttered Kennington in disbelief.

"Hardly excessive," suggested Max, "remembering that a complete set could fetch more than a million—" he paused—"or nothing, were your brother to acquire the red king."

"I take your point," repeated Kennington. "But you still might be able to pick it up for a few hundred dollars."

"Let's hope so," said Max.

Max Glover left White's Club a few minutes after three, explaining to his host that he had another appointment that afternoon, which indeed he did.

Max checked his watch and decided he still had enough time to stroll through Green Park and not be late for his next meeting.

Max arrived in Sloane Square a few minutes before four, and took a seat on a bench opposite the statue of Sir Francis Drake. He began to rehearse his new script. When he heard the clock on a nearby tower chime four times, he leaped up and walked briskly across to Cadogan Square. He stopped at No 16, climbed the steps, and rang the doorbell.

James Kennington opened the door and greeted his guest with a smile.

"I rang earlier this morning," explained Max. "My name's Glover."

James Kennington ushered him through to the drawing room and offered Max a seat by an unlit fire. The younger brother took the seat opposite him.

Although the apartment was spacious, even grand, there were one or two clear outlines on the walls to suggest where pictures had once hung. Max suspected that they were not being cleaned or reframed. Gossip columns regularly referred to the Hon. James's drinking habits and hinted at several unpaid gambling debts.

When Max came to the end of his tale, he was well prepared for the Hon. James's first question.

"How much do you imagine the piece will fetch, Mr. Glover?"

"A few hundred dollars," Max replied. "That's assuming your brother doesn't find out about the auction." He paused, sipped his tea, and added, "In excess of fifty thousand, if he does."

"But I don't have fifty thousand," said James, something else Max was well aware of. "And if my brother were to find out," James continued, "there would be nothing I could do about it. The terms of the will couldn't be clearer—whoever finds the red king inherits the set."

"I'd be willing to put up the necessary capital to secure the piece," said Max, not missing a beat, "if in turn you would then agree to sell me the set."

"And how much would you be willing to pay?" asked James.

"Half a million," said Max.

"But Sotheby's have already valued a complete set at over a million," protested James.

"That may well be the case," said Max, "but half a million is surely better than nothing, which would be the outcome if your brother were to learn of the red king's existence."

"But you said that the red king might sell for a few hundred—"

"In which case, I would require only a

thousand pounds in advance, against two and a half percent of the hammer price," said Max for the second time that afternoon.

"That's a risk I am quite willing to take," said James with the smile of someone who believes he has gained the upper hand. "If the red king should sell for less than fifty thousand," he continued, "I'd be able to raise the money myself. If it goes for more than fifty thousand, you can purchase the piece and I'll sell you the set for half a million." James sipped his tea, before adding, "I can't lose either way."

Neither can I, thought Max, as he extracted a contract from an inside pocket. James read the document slowly. He looked up and said, "You obviously felt confident that I would fall in with your plan, Mr. Glover."

"If you hadn't," said Max, "my next visit would have been to your brother, which would have left you with nothing. At least now, to quote you, you can't lose either way."

"Presumably I will have to travel to New York," said James.

"Not necessary," replied Max. "You can

bid for the piece by phone, which has the added advantage that no one else will know who's on the other end of the line."

"But how do I go about that?" asked James.

"It couldn't be easier," Max assured him. "The New York sale begins at two in the afternoon, which will be seven o'clock in the evening in London. The red king is lot twenty-three, so I'll arrange for Phillips to place a call through to you once they reach lot twenty-one. Just be sure you're sitting by the phone, with no one else blocking the line."

"And you'll take over, if it goes above fifty thousand?"

"You have my word," said Max, looking him straight in the eye.

Max flew to New York the weekend before the sale was due to take place. He booked himself into a small hotel on the East Side and settled for a room not much larger than our cell, but then he only had enough money left over to cover the endgame.

Max rose early on the Monday morning. He hadn't been able to sleep because of an orchestra of New York traffic and police sirens. He used the time to go over and over the different permutations that might occur once the sale began. He would be on center stage for less than two minutes and, if he failed, would be back on the next plane to Heathrow, with nothing to show for his efforts other than an overdrawn bank account.

He grabbed a bagel on the corner of Third and 66th, before walking another few blocks to Phillips. He spent the rest of the morning at a manuscript sale that was being held in the room where the Chinese auction would take place. He sat silently at the back of the room, watching how the Americans conduct an auction, so that he wouldn't be wrong-footed later that afternoon.

Max didn't eat any lunch, and not just because his meager funds were already stretched to their limit. Instead, he used the time to make two overseas calls; the first to Lord Kennington, to confirm that he still had his authority to take the bidding for the red king up to fifty thousand dollars. Max assured him that, the moment the hammer fell, he would call to let him know what sum the piece had sold for. A few minutes later

Max made a second call, this time to the Hon. James Kennington at his home in Cadogan Square. James picked up the phone after one ring, clearly relieved to hear Max's voice on the other end of the line. Max made the Hon. James Kennington exactly the same promise.

Max replaced the phone and made his way across to the bidding counter, where he gave an assistant the details of James Kennington's telephone number in London and told her of his intention to bid for Lot 23.

"Leave it to us, sir," the assistant replied. "I'll make sure we're in touch with him well in time."

Max thanked the assistant, made his way back to the saleroom and took his favored place on the end of the eighth row, just to the right of the auctioneer. He began to turn the pages of the catalog, checking on items in which he had no interest. While he sat around, impatiently waiting for the auctioneer to invite bids for lot number one, he tried to work out who were the dealers, who the serious bidders and who the simply curious.

By the time the auctioneer climbed the steps of the rostrum at five minutes to two, the saleroom was full of expectant faces. At two o'clock the auctioneer smiled down at his clientele.

"Lot number one," he declared, "a delicately crafted ivory fisherman."

The piece sold for $850, giving no hint of the drama that was about to follow.

Lot 2 reached $1,000, but it wasn't until Lot 17, the figure of a mandarin bent over a desk reading a ledger, that the $5,000 mark was achieved.

One or two dealers whose only interest was clearly in later lots began to drift into the room, while a couple of others left, having failed or succeeded in acquiring the items they'd been after. Max could hear his heart pounding, although it would still be some time before the auctioneer reached Lot 23.

He turned his attention to the row of phones on a long table by the side of the room. Only three were manned. When the auctioneer called Lot 21, an assistant started to dial. A few moments later, she cupped a hand over the mouthpiece and began to whisper. When Lot 22 was offered, she spoke briefly to her client again. Max assumed that she must be warning James

Kennington that the red king would be the next item to come under the hammer.

"Lot twenty-three," declared the auctioneer glancing down at his notes. "An exquisitely carved red king, provenance unknown. Do I have an opening bid of three hundred dollars?"

Max raised his catalog.

"Five hundred?" inquired the auctioneer turning to face the assistant on the phone. She whispered into the mouthpiece and then nodded firmly. The auctioneer turned his attention back to Max, who had raised his catalog even before a price had been suggested.

"I have a bid of a thousand dollars," said the auctioneer, returning to face the telephone bidder. "Two thousand," he ventured, surprised to see the assistant nod so quickly.

"Three thousand?" he suggested as he looked back at Max. The catalog shot up again, and several dealers at the back of the room began chatting among themselves.

"Four thousand?" inquired the auctioneer, staring in disbelief at the assistant on the phone. $5,000, $6,000, $7,000, $8,000, $9,000 and $10,000 were overtaken in less than a minute. The auctioneer tried desperately to look as if this was exactly what he had anticipated as the murmurs in the room grew louder and louder. Everyone seemed to have an opinion. One or two dealers abandoned their favored places and quickly walked to the back of the room, hoping to find an explanation for the bidding frenzy. Some were already beginning to make assumptions, but were in no position to bid under such pressure, especially as the amounts were now going up in leaps of $5,000.

Max raised his catalog in response to the auctioneer's inquiry, "Forty-five thousand? Are you bidding fifty thousand?" he inquired of the lady on the telephone. Everyone in the room turned to see how she would respond. For the first time she hesitated. The auctioneer repeated, "Fifty thousand." She whispered the figure into the phone and, after a long pause, nodded, but not quite so enthusiastically.

When Max was offered the piece for $55,000, he also hesitated, taking his time before he finally raised his catalog.

"Sixty thousand?" suggested the auctioneer to the assistant on the phone. Max waited nervously as she cupped her hand over the mouthpiece and repeated the figure. Beads of sweat began to appear on Max's forehead, as he wondered if James Kennington had managed to raise more than $50,000, in which case he would just about clear his expenses on the whole exercise. After what seemed like an eternity, but was, in fact, only twenty seconds, the assistant shook her head. She put the phone down.

When the auctioneer smiled in Max's direction and said, "Sold to the gentleman on my left, for fifty-five thousand dollars," Max felt sick, triumphant, dazed and relieved all at the same time.

Max remained in his place, as he waited for the furor to die down. After a dozen more lots had been disposed of, he slipped quietly out of the room, unaware of the suspicious stares from dealers, who wondered who he was. He strolled across the thick green carpet and stopped at the purchasing counter.

"I wish to leave a deposit on lot twenty-three."

The clerk looked down at her list. "A red king," she said, and double-checked the price. "Fifty-five thousand dollars," she added, and looked up at Max for confirmation.

He nodded as the assistant began to fill in the little boxes on the purchasing document. A few moments later she swiveled the form round for Max to sign.

"That will be five thousand, five hundred dollars deposit," she said, "and the full amount must be settled within twenty-eight days." Max nodded nonchalantly, as if this was a procedure he was well familiar with. He signed the agreement and then wrote out a check for $5,500, aware that it would empty his account. He pushed it across the counter. The assistant handed him back the top copy of the agreement and retained the duplicate. When she checked the signature, she hesitated. It might have been a coincidence: after all, Glover was a common enough name. She didn't want to insult a customer, but she knew she would have to report the anomaly to their compliance department, before they could consider cashing the check.

Max left the auction house and headed north to Park Avenue. He strode confidently into Sotheby Parke Bernet and approached the reception desk. He asked if he could have a word with the Head of the Oriental Department. He was kept waiting for only a few minutes.

On this occasion, Max didn't waste time

with any preliminary questions that would have only been a smokescreen to disguise his true intent. After all, as the sales clerk at Phillips had pointed out, he only had twenty-eight days to complete the transaction.

"Should the Kennington Chess Set come onto the market, what would you expect it to fetch?" Max asked.

The expert looked incredulous, although he had already been briefed on the sale of the red king at Phillips, and on the price the piece had fetched. "Seven hundred and fifty thousand, possibly as much as a million," came back the reply.

"And if I was able to deliver the Kennington Set, and you were in a position to authenticate it, what amount would Sotheby's be willing to advance against a future sale?"

"Four hundred thousand, possibly five, if the family were able to confirm that it was the Kennington Set."

"I'll be in touch," promised Max, all his immediate and long-term problems solved.

Max checked out of his little hotel on the East Side later that evening, and took a taxi to

Kennedy Airport. Once the plane had taken off, he slept soundly for the first time in days.

The 727 touched down at Heathrow just as the sun was rising over the Thames. Having nothing to declare, Max took the Heathrow Express to Paddington, and was back in his flat in time for breakfast. He began to fantasize about what it would be like to dine regularly at his favorite restaurant and always hail a taxi, rather than having to wait for the next bus.

Once he'd finished breakfast, Max put the plates in the sink and settled down in the one comfortable chair. He began to consider his next move, confident that now the red king had found its place on the board, the game must end in checkmate.

At eleven o'clock—a proper hour to phone a peer of the realm—Max put a call through to Kennington Hall. When the butler transferred the call to Lord Kennington, his first words were, "Did we get it?"

"Unfortunately not, my lord," replied Max. "We were outbid by an unknown party. I carried out your instructions to the letter, and stopped bidding at fifty thousand dollars." He paused. "The hammer price was fifty-five thousand."

There was a long silence. "Do you think the other bidder could have been my brother?"

"I've no way of knowing," replied Max. "All I can tell you is that they were bidding by phone, no doubt wishing to ensure their anonymity."

"I'll find out soon enough," responded Kennington, before hanging up.

"You certainly will," agreed Max as he began to dial a number in Chelsea.

"Congratulations," said Max the moment he heard the Hon. James's plummy voice. "I've purchased the piece, so you're now in a position to claim your inheritance, under the terms of the will."

"Well done, Glover," said James Kennington.

"And the moment you deliver the rest of the set, my lawyers have been instructed to hand over a check for four hundred and forty-five thousand dollars," said Max.

"But we agreed on half a million," snapped James.

"Minus the fifty-five thousand I had to pay for the red king." Max paused. "You'll find it's all spelled out in the contract."

"But—" James began to protest.

"Would you prefer me to call your brother?" Max asked, as the front door bell rang. "Because I'm still in possession of the piece." James didn't immediately reply. "Think about it," added Max, "while I answer the front door." Max placed the receiver on the side table, and strolled out into the hall, almost rubbing his hands. He released the chain, undid the Yale lock, and pulled the door open a couple of inches. Two tall men wearing identical trench coats stood in front of him.

"Max Victor Glover?" inquired one of them.

"Who wants to know?" asked Max.

"I'm Detective Inspector Armitage of the Fraud Squad, and this is Detective Sergeant Willis." They both produced warrant cards, with which Max was only too familiar. "May we come in, sir?"

Once the police had taken down Max's statement, which consisted of little more than, "I'll need to speak to my solicitor," the two men departed. They then drove up to Yorkshire for a meeting with Lord Kennington. Having obtained a detailed statement from his lordship, they returned to London to interview his brother James. The police found him just as co-operative.

A week later Max was arrested for fraud. The judge took into account his past blemished record, and did not grant bail.

"But how did they find out that you'd stolen the red king?" I asked.

"They didn't," Max replied as he stubbed out his cigarette.

I put my pen down. "I'm not sure I understand," I murmured from the upper bunk.

"And neither did I," admitted Max, "at least not until they charged me." I remained silent, as my pad mate began to roll his next cigarette. "When they read out the charge sheet," he continued, " no one was more surprised than me.

"'Max Victor Glover, you are charged with attempting to obtain money by false pretenses. Namely that on October seventeenth, two thousand, you bid fifty-five thousand dollars for a red king, lot twenty-three at Phillips auctioneers in New York, while enticing other interested parties to bid against you, without informing them that you were the owner of the piece.'"

A heavy key turned in the lock and our cell door cranked open.

"Visits," bellowed the wing officer.

"So you see," said Max as he swung his legs off the bunk, "I was charged with the wrong offense, and sentenced for the wrong crime."

"But why go through such an elaborate charade, when you could have sold the red king to either of the brothers?"

"Because then I would have had to show them how I got hold of the piece in the first place, and if I had been caught . . ."

"But you were caught."

"But not charged with theft," Max reminded me.

"So what happened to the red king?" I demanded, as we stepped out into the corridor and made our way across to the visits center.

"It was returned to my solicitor after the trial," said Max, "and locked up in his safe, where it will remain until I'm released."

"But that means—" I began.

"Have you ever met Lord Kennington?" Max asked casually.

"No, I haven't," I replied.

"Then I'll introduce you, old boy," he mimicked, "because he's coming to visit me this afternoon." Max paused. "I have a feeling that his lordship is about to make me an offer for the red king."

"And will you accept his offer?" I asked.

"Steady on, Jeff," Max replied as we entered the visits room. "I won't be able to answer that question until next week, when I've had a visit from his brother James."

The Wisdom of Solomon

"Mind your own business," was Carol's advice.

"But it is my business," I reminded my wife as I climbed into bed. "Bob and I have been friends for over twenty years."

"All the more reason to keep your own counsel," she insisted.

"But I don't like her," I replied tartly.

"You made that abundantly clear during dinner," Carol reminded me as she switched off her bedside light.

"But surely you can see that it's going to end in tears."

"Then you'll just have to buy a large box of Kleenex."

"She's only after his money," I muttered.

"He hasn't got any," replied Carol. "Bob's practice is quite successful, but hardly puts him in the Abramovich league."

"That may well be the case, but it's still my duty, as a friend, to warn him not to marry her."

"He doesn't want to hear that at the moment," said Carol, "so don't even think about it."

"Explain to me, O wise one," I said as I plumped up my pillow, "why not."

Carol ignored my sarcasm. "If it should end up in the divorce courts, you'll just look smug. If the marriage turns out to be wedded bliss, he'll never forgive you—and neither will she."

"I wasn't planning to tell her."

"She already knows exactly how you feel about her," said Carol. "Believe me."

"It won't last a year," I predicted, just as the phone rang on my side of the bed. I picked it up, praying it wasn't a patient.

"I've only got one question for you," said a voice that needed no introduction.

"And what's that, Bob?" I asked.
"Will you be my best man?"

Bob Radford and I first met at St. Thomas' Hospital when we were both house officers. To be more accurate, we had first come into contact with each other on the rugby field, when he tackled me just as I thought I was about to score the winning try. In those days we were on opposite sides.

After we were appointed senior house officers at Guy's, we started playing for the same rugby team and regularly had a midweek game of squash—which he invariably won. In our final year we ended up sharing digs in Lambeth. We didn't need to look far for female companionship as St. Thomas' had over three thousand nurses, most of whom wanted sex and for some unfathomable reason considered doctors a safe bet. Both of us looked forward to taking advantage of our new status. And then I fell in love.

Carol was also a house officer at Guy's, and on our first date made it abundantly clear that she wasn't looking for a long-term relationship. However, she underestimated my one talent, persistence. She finally gave in after I'd proposed for the ninth time. Carol and I were married a few months after she'd qualified.

Bob headed off in the opposite direction. Whenever we invited him to dinner, he would turn up escorted by a new companion. I sometimes got their names muddled up, a mistake Carol never made. However, as the years passed, even Bob's appetite to taste some new delicacy from the table d'hôte became less hearty than it had been during his student days; after all, we had both recently celebrated our fortieth birthdays. It didn't help when Bob was named in the student rag as the most eligible bachelor in the hospital, not least because he had built up one of the most successful private practices in London. He had a set of rooms in Harley Street, with none of the expenses associated with marital bliss. But now that finally seemed to be coming to an end.

When Bob invited Carol and me to join him for dinner so that he could introduce us to Fiona, whom he described as the woman he was going to spend the rest of his life with, we were both surprised and delighted. We were also a little perplexed as we couldn't recall the name of his last girlfriend. We were fairly confident it wasn't Fiona.

When we arrived at the restaurant, we saw the two of them seated in the far corner of the room, holding hands. Bob rose to greet us and immediately introduced Fiona as the most wonderful girl in the world. To be fair to the woman, no red-blooded male could have denied Fiona's physical attributes. She must have been about five foot nine, made up of thirty inches of leg, attached to a figure honed in the gym and no doubt perfected on a diet of lettuce leaves and water.

Our conversation during the meal was fairly limited, partly because Bob spent most of the time staring at Fiona in a way that should be reserved for one of Donatello's nudes. By the end of the meal, I had come to the conclusion that Fiona would end up costing about as much, and it wasn't just because she read the wine list from the bottom upward, ordered caviar as a starter and asked, with a sweet smile, for her pasta to be covered in truffles.

Frankly, Fiona was the type of long-legged blonde whom you hope to bump into, while perched on a stool in a hotel bar, late at night and preferably on another continent. I am unable to tell you how old she was, but I did learn during dinner that she had been married three times before she met Bob. However, she assured us that, this time, she had found the right man.

I was only too happy to escape that night and, as you have already discovered, I didn't waste much time making my wife aware of my views on Fiona.

The marriage took place some three months later at the Chelsea Register Office in the King's Road. The ceremony was attended by several of Bob's friends from St. Thomas' and Guy's—some of whom I hadn't set eyes on since our rugby days. I felt it unwise to point out to Carol that Fiona didn't seem to have any friends, or at least none who were willing to attend her latest nuptials.

I stood silently by Bob's side as the registrar intoned the words, "If anyone can show lawful reason why these two should not be joined in matrimony, then they should declare that reason to me now."

I wanted to offer an opinion, but Carol was too close at hand to risk it. I must confess that Fiona did look radiant on that occasion, not unlike a python about to devour a lamb—whole.

The reception was held at Lucio's on the Fulham Road. The best man's speech might have been more coherent if I hadn't consumed quite so much champagne, or if I'd believed a word I was uttering.

When I sat down to indulgent applause, Carol didn't lean across to congratulate me. I avoided her until we all joined the bride and groom on the pavement outside the restaurant. Bob and Fiona waved goodbye before stepping into a white stretch limousine that would take them to Heathrow. From there, they were to board a plane to Acapulco, where they would spend a three-week honeymoon. Neither the transport to Heathrow, which incidentally could have accommodated the entire wedding party, nor the final destination for the honeymoon, had been Bob's first choice. A piece of information I didn't pass on to Carol, as she would undoubtedly have accused me of being prejudiced—and she would have been right.

I can't pretend that I saw a lot of Fiona during their first year of marriage, although Bob called from time to time, but only from his practice in Harley Street. We even managed the occasional lunch, but he no longer seemed to be able to fit in a game of squash in the evening.

Over lunch Bob never failed to expound the virtues of his remarkable wife, as if only too aware of my attitude to his spouse— although I never at any time expressed my true feelings. I could only assume that this was the reason Carol and I were never invited to dinner at their home, and whenever we asked them to join us for supper, Bob made some unconvincing excuse about having to visit a patient, or being out of town on that particular evening.

The change was subtle to begin with, almost imperceptible. Our lunches became more regular, even the occasional game of squash was fitted in, and perhaps more relevant, there were fewer and fewer references to Fiona's pending sainthood.

It was soon after the death of Bob's aunt, a Miss Muriel Pembleton, that the change became far less subtle. To be honest, I didn't even realize that Bob had an aunt, let alone one who was the sole heir to Pembleton Electronics.

The Times revealed that Miss Pembleton had left a little over seven million pounds in shares and property, as well as a considerable art collection. With the exception of a few minor bequests to charitable organizations, her nephew turned out to be the sole beneficiary. God bless the man, because coming into an unexpected fortune didn't change Bob in any way; but the same couldn't be said of Fiona.

When I called Bob to congratulate him on his good fortune, he sounded very low. He asked if I could possibly join him for lunch, as he needed to seek my advice on a personal matter.

We met a couple of hours later, at a gastro pub just off Devonshire Place. Bob didn't talk about anything consequential until after the waiter had taken our order, but once the first course had been served, Fiona was the only other dish on the menu. He had received a letter that morning from Abbott Crombie & Co, Solicitors, stating, in unambiguous terms, that his wife was filing for divorce.

"Can't fault her timing," I said tactlessly.

"And I didn't even spot it," said Bob.

"Spot it?" I repeated. "Spot what?"

"How Fiona's attitude to me changed not long after she'd met my aunt Muriel. In fact, that same night, she literally charmed the pants off me."

I reminded Bob of what Woody Allen had said on the subject. Mr. Allen could not understand why God had given man a penis and a brain, but not enough blood to connect the two. Bob laughed for the first time that day, but it was only moments before he lapsed back into a maudlin silence.

"Is there anything I can do to help?" I asked.

"Only if you know the name of a first-class divorce lawyer," Bob replied, "because I'm told that Mrs. Abbott has a reputation for extracting the last drop of blood on behalf of her clients, especially following the latest law lords' ruling in favor of spouses."

"Can't say I do," I responded. "Having been happily married for sixteen years, I fear I'm the wrong man to advise you. Why don't you have a word with Peter Mitchell? After all, with four ex-wives, he ought to be able to tell you who's the best advocate available."

"I called Peter first thing this morning," admitted Bob. "He's always been represented by Mrs. Abbott—told me that he keeps her on a permanent retainer."

During the next few weeks, Bob and I returned to the squash court regularly, and I started beating him for the first time. He would then join Carol and me for dinner afterward. We tried to steer clear of any talk about Fiona. However, he did let slip that she was refusing to leave the stage grace-

fully, even after he had offered her half of Aunt Muriel's bequest.

As the weeks turned into months, Bob began losing weight and his golden locks were turning prematurely gray. Fiona, on the other hand, seemed to go from strength to strength, taking each new hurdle like a sea-

soned thoroughbred. When it came to tac-
tics, Fiona clearly understood the long
game, but then she had the advantage of
having experienced three away victories,
and was clearly looking forward to a fourth.

It must have been about a year later that
Fiona finally agreed to a settlement. All of
Bob's assets were to be divided equally between them, while he would also cover her
legal costs. A date was set for a formal signing in chambers. I agreed to act as a witness and give Bob, as Carol described it,
much-needed moral support.

I never even took the top off my pen because Fiona burst into tears long before
Mrs. Abbott had read out the terms, declaring that she was being cruelly treated and
Bob was causing her to have a nervous
breakdown. She then flounced out of the office without another word. I must confess
that I had never seen Fiona looking less nervous. Even Mrs. Abbott couldn't hide her
exasperation.

Harry Dexter, whom Bob had selected as
his solicitor, warned him that this was likely
to end up in a lengthy and expensive courtroom battle if he couldn't agree to a settle-

ment. Mr. Dexter added, for good measure, that judges often instruct the defending party to shoulder the injured party's costs. Bob shrugged his shoulders, not even bothering to respond.

Once both sides had accepted that an out-of-court settlement could not be reached, a day was fixed in the judge's calendar for a hearing.

Mr. Dexter was determined to counter Fiona's outrageous demands with equally fierce resistance, and to begin with Bob went along with all his recommendations. But with each new demand from the other side, Bob's resolve began to weaken until, like a punch-drunk boxer, he was ready to throw in the towel. He became more and more depressed as the day of the hearing drew nearer, and even began saying, "Why don't I just give her everything because that's the only way she'll ever be satisfied?" Carol and I tried to lift his spirits, but with little success, and even Mr. Dexter was finding it harder and harder to convince his client to hang in there.

We both assured Bob that we would be

in court to support him on the day of the hearing.

Carol and I took our places in the gallery of court number three, matrimonial division, on the last Thursday in June, and waited for proceedings to begin. By ten to ten the court officials began to drift in and take their places. A few minutes later Mrs. Abbott arrived, with Fiona by her side. I stared down at the plaintiff, who was wearing no jewelry and a black suit that would have been more appropriate for a funeral—Bob's.

A moment later Mr. Dexter appeared with Bob in his wake. They took their places at a table on the other side of the courtroom.

As ten o'clock struck, my worst fears were realized. The judge entered the courtroom—a woman who immediately brought back memories of my old school matron—a martinet who didn't believe that the punishment should fit the crime. The judge took her place on the bench and smiled down at Mrs. Abbott. They'd probably been at university together. Mrs. Abbott rose from her place and returned the judge's smile. She then proceeded to do battle for every jot and tittle in Bob's possession, even arguing over who should end up with his college cufflinks, saying that it had been agreed that all Mr. Radford's assets should be divided equally, so that if he had one cufflink, her client must be entitled to the other.

As each hour passed, Fiona's demands expanded. After all, Mrs. Abbot explained, hadn't her client given up a rewarding and happy lifestyle in America, which included a thriving family business—something I'd never heard mentioned before—to devote herself to her husband? Only to discover that he rarely arrived home in the evening before eight, and then only after he'd been out with his friends to play squash, and when he eventually turned up—Mrs. Abbott paused—drunk, he didn't want to eat the meal she had spent hours preparing for him—she paused again— and when they later went to bed, he quickly fell into a drunken slumber. I rose from my place in the gallery to protest, only to be told by an usher to sit down or I would be asked to leave the court. Carol tugged firmly on my jacket.

Finally, Mrs. Abbot reached the end of

her demands, with the suggestion that her client should be given their home in the country (Aunt Muriel's), while Bob would be allowed to keep his London apartment; she should have the villa in Cannes (Aunt Muriel's), while he kept his rooms at Harley Street (rented). Mrs. Abbott finally turned her attention to Aunt Muriel's art collection, which she also felt should be divided equally; her client should have the Monet, while he kept the Manguin. She should have the Picasso, he the Pasmore, she the Bacon, etc. When Mrs. Abbott finally sat down, Mrs. Justice Butler suggested that perhaps they should take a break for lunch.

During a lunch, not eaten, Mr. Dexter, Carol and I tried valiantly to convince Bob that he should fight back. But he wouldn't hear of it.

"If I can hold on to everything I had before my aunt died," Bob insisted, "that will be quite enough for me."

Mr. Dexter felt certain he could do far better than that, but Bob showed little interest in putting up a fight.

"Just get it over with," he instructed. "Try not to forget who's paying her costs."

When we returned to the courtroom at

two o'clock that afternoon, the judge turned her attention to Bob's solicitor.

"And what do you have to say about all this, Mr. Dexter?" asked Mrs. Justice Butler.

"We are happy to go along with the division of my client's assets as suggested by Mrs. Abbott," he replied with an exaggerated sigh.

"You're happy to go along with Mrs. Abbott's recommendations, Mr. Dexter?" repeated the judge in disbelief.

Once again Mr. Dexter looked at Bob, who simply nodded, like a dog on the back shelf of a car.

"So be it," said Mrs. Justice Butler, unable to mask her surprise.

She was just about to pass judgment, when Fiona broke down and burst into tears. She leaned across and whispered into Mrs. Abbott's ear.

"Mrs. Abbott," said Mrs. Justice Butler, ignoring the plaintiff's sobs, "am I to sanction this agreement?"

"It seems not," said Mrs. Abbott, rising from her place and looking somewhat embarrassed. "It appears that my client still feels that such a settlement favors the defendant."

"Does she indeed?" said Mrs. Justice Butler and turned to face Fiona. Mrs. Abbott touched her client on the shoulder and whispered in her ear. Fiona immediately rose, and kept her head bowed while the judge spoke.

"Mrs. Radford," she began, looking down at Fiona, "am I to understand that you are no longer happy with the settlement your solicitor has secured for you?"

Fiona nodded demurely.

"Then may I suggest a solution, that I hope will bring this case to a speedy conclusion." Fiona looked up and smiled sweetly at the judge, while Bob sank lower into his seat.

"Perhaps it would be easier, Mrs. Radford, if *you* were to draw up two lists for the court's consideration, that *you* believe to be a fair and equitable division of your husband's assets?"

"I'd be happy to do that, your honor," said Fiona meekly.

"Does this meet with your approval, Mr. Dexter?" asked Mrs. Justice Butler, turning back to Bob's solicitor.

"Yes, m'lady," said Mr. Dexter, trying not to sound exasperated.

"Can I take it that those are your client's instructions?"

Mr. Dexter glanced down at Bob, who didn't even bother to offer an opinion.

"And Mrs. Abbott," she said, turning her attention back to Fiona's solicitor, "I want your word that your client will not back down from such a settlement."

"I can assure you, m'lady, that she will comply with your ruling," replied Fiona's solicitor.

"So be it," said Mrs. Justice Butler. "We will adjourn until tomorrow morning at ten o'clock, when I will look forward to considering Mrs. Radford's two lists."

Carol and I took Bob out for dinner that night—a pointless exercise. He rarely opened his mouth to either eat or speak.

"Let her have everything," he finally ventured over coffee, "because that's the only way I'm ever going to be rid of the woman."

"But your aunt wouldn't have left you her fortune if she'd known this would have been the eventual outcome."

"Neither Aunt Muriel nor I worked that one out," Bob replied with resignation. "And you can't fault Fiona's timing. She only needed another month after meeting my dear aunt before she accepted my proposal." Bob turned and stared at me, an accusing look in his eyes. "Why didn't you warn me not to marry her?" he demanded.

When the judge entered the courtroom the following morning all the officials were already in place. The two adversaries were seated next to their solicitors. All those in the well of the court rose and bowed as Mrs. Justice Butler resumed her place, leaving only Mrs. Abbott on her feet.

"Has your client had enough time to prepare her two lists?" inquired the judge, as she stared down at Fiona's counsel.

"She has indeed, m'lady," said Mrs. Abbott, "and both are ready for your consideration."

The judge nodded to the clerk of the court. He walked slowly across to Mrs. Abbott, who handed over the two lists. The clerk then walked slowly back to the bench and passed them up to the judge for her consideration.

Mrs. Justice Butler took her time studying the two inventories, occasionally nodding, even adding the odd "Um," while Mrs.

Abbott remained on her feet. Once the judge had reached the last items on the lists, she turned her attention back to counsel's bench.

"Am I to understand," inquired Mrs. Justice Butler, "that both parties consider this to be a fair and equitable distribution of all the assets in question?"

"Yes, m'lady," said Mrs. Abbott firmly, on behalf of her client.

"I see," said the judge and, turning to Mr. Dexter, asked, "Does this also meet with your client's approval?"

Mr. Dexter hesitated. "Yes, m'lady," he eventually managed, unable to mask the irony in his voice.

"So be it." Fiona smiled for the first time since the case had opened. The judge returned her smile. "However, before I pass judgment," she continued, "I still have one question for Mr. Radford." Bob glanced at his solicitor before rising nervously from his seat. He looked up at the judge.

What more can she want? was my only thought as I sat staring down from the gallery.

"Mr. Radford," began the judge, "we have all heard your wife tell the court that she considers these two lists to be a fair and equitable division of all your assets."

Bob bowed his head and remained silent.

"However, before I pass judgment, I need to be sure that you agree with that assessment."

Bob raised his head. He seemed to hesitate a moment, but then said, "I do, m'lady."

"Then I am left with no choice in this matter," declared Mrs. Justice Butler. She paused, and stared directly down at Fiona, who was still smiling. "As I allowed Mrs. Radford the opportunity to prepare these two lists," continued the judge, "which in her judgment are an equitable and fair division of your assets—" Mrs. Justice Butler was pleased to see Fiona nodding her agreement—"then it must also be fair and equitable," the judge added, turning her attention back to Bob, "to allow Mr. Radford the opportunity to select which of the two lists he would prefer."

Know What
I Mean?

"If you wanna find out what's goin' on in this nick, I'm the man to 'ave a word with," said Doug. "Know what I mean?"

Every prison has one. At North Sea Camp his name was Doug Haslett. Doug was half an inch under six foot, with thick, black, wavy hair that was going gray at the temples, and a stomach that hung out over his trousers. Doug's idea of exercise was the walk from the library, where he was the prison orderly, to the canteen a hundred yards away, three times a day. I think he exercised his mind at about the same pace.

It didn't take me long to discover that he

was bright, cunning, manipulative and lazy—traits that are common among recidivists. Within days of arriving at a new prison, Doug could be guaranteed to have procured fresh clothes, the best cell, the highest paid job, and to have worked out which prisoners, and—more important—which officers he needed to get on the right side of.

As I spent a lot of my free time in the library—and it was rarely overcrowded, despite the prison accommodating over four hundred inmates—Doug quickly made me aware of his case history. Some prisoners, when they discover that you're a writer, clam up. Others can't stop talking. Despite the silence notices displayed all around the library, Doug fell into the latter category.

When Doug left school at the age of seventeen, the only exam he passed was his driving test—first time. Four years later he added a heavy goods license to his qualifications, and at the same time landed his first job as a lorry driver.

Doug quickly became disillusioned with how little he could earn, traipsing backward and forward to the south of France with a load of Brussels sprouts and peas, often returning to Sleaford with an empty lorry and therefore no bonus. He regularly fouled up (his words) when it came to EU regulations, and took the view that somehow he was exempt from having to pay tax. He blamed the French for too much unnecessary red tape and a Labor government for punitive taxes. When the courts finally served a debt order on him, everyone was to blame except Doug.

The bailiff took away all his possessions— except the lorry, which Doug was still paying for on a hire-purchase agreement.

Doug was just about to pack in being a lorry driver and join the dole queue—almost as remunerative, and you don't have to get up in the morning—when he was approached by a man he'd never come across before, while on a stopover in Marseilles. Doug was having breakfast at a dockside cafe when the man slid on to the stool next to him. The stranger didn't waste any time with introductions, he came straight to the point. Doug listened with interest; after all, he had already dumped his cargo of sprouts and peas on the dockside, and had been expecting to return home with an empty lorry. All Doug had to do, the stranger assured him, was to deliver a consignment of bananas to Lincolnshire once a week.

I feel I should point out that Doug did have some scruples. He made it clear to his new employer that he would never be willing to transport drugs, and wouldn't even discuss illegal immigrants. Doug, like so many of my fellow inmates, was very right wing.

When Doug arrived at the drop-off point, a derelict barn deep in the Lincolnshire countryside, he was handed a thick brown envelope containing £25,000 in cash. They didn't even expect him to help unload the produce.

Overnight, Doug's lifestyle changed.

After a couple of trips, Doug began to work part-time, making the single journey to Marseilles and back once a week. Despite this, he was now earning more in a week than he was declaring on his tax return for a year.

Doug decided that one of the things he'd do with his new-found wealth was to move out of his basement flat on the Hinton Road and invest in the property market.

Over the next month he was shown around several properties in Sleaford, accompanied by a young lady from one of the local estate agents. Sally McKenzie was puzzled how a lorry driver could possibly afford the type of properties she was offering him.

Doug eventually settled on a little cottage on the outskirts of Sleaford. Sally was even more surprised when he put down the deposit in cash, and shocked when he asked her out on a date.

Six months later Sally moved in with Doug, although it still worried her that she couldn't work out where all the money was coming from.

Doug's sudden wealth created other problems that he hadn't anticipated. What do you do with £25,000 in cash each week, when you can't open a bank account, or pay a monthly check into a building society? The basement flat on Hinton Road had been replaced with a cottage in the country. The secondhand fork-lift truck had been traded in for a sixteen-wheel Mercedes lorry. The annual holiday at a bed and breakfast in Blackpool had been upgraded to a rented villa in the Algarve. The Portuguese seemed quite happy to accept cash, whatever the currency.

On their second visit to the Algarve a year later, Doug fell on one knee, proposed to Sally and presented her with a diamond engagement ring the size of an acorn: traditional sort of chap, Doug.

Several people, not least his young wife, remained puzzled as to how Doug could possibly afford such a lifestyle while only earning £25,000 a year. "Cash bonuses for overtime," was all he came up with whenever Sally asked. This surprised Mrs. Haslett because she knew that her husband only worked a couple of days a week. And she might never have found out the truth if someone else hadn't taken an interest.

Mark Cainen, an ambitious young assistant officer with HM Customs, decided the time had come to check exactly what Doug was importing, after a narc tipped him off it might not just be bananas.

When Doug was returning from one of his weekly trips to Marseilles, Mr. Cainen asked him to pull over and park his lorry in the customs shed. Doug climbed down from the cab and handed over his worksheet to the officer. Bananas were the only entry on the manifest: fifty crates of them. The young customs official set about opening the crates one by one, and by the time he'd reached the thirty-sixth, was beginning to wonder if he had been given a bum steer; that opinion changed when he opened the forty-first crate, which was packed tightly with cigarettes—Marlboro, Benson & Hedges, Silk Cut and Players. By the time Mr. Cainen had opened the fiftieth crate, he had placed an estimated street value on the contraband of over £200,000.

"I had no idea what was in those crates," Doug assured his wife, and she believed him. He repeated the same story to his defense team, who wanted to believe him, and for a third time, to the jury, who didn't. Doug's defense silk reminded his lordship that this was Mr. Haslett's first offense and his wife was expecting a baby. The judge listened in stony silence, and sent Doug down for four years.

Doug spent his first week in Lincoln high-security prison, but once he'd completed an induction form and was able to place a tick in all the right boxes—no drugs, no violence, no previous offenses—he was quickly transferred to an open prison.

At North Sea Camp, Doug, as I've already explained, opted to work in the library. The alternatives were the pig farm, the kitchen, the stores or cleaning out the lavatories. Doug quickly discovered that despite there being over four hundred residents in the prison, as librarian he was on to a cushy number. His income fell from £25,000 a week to £12.50, of which he spent £10 on phone cards so that he could keep in touch with his pregnant wife.

Doug rang Sally twice a week—you can only phone out when you're in prison, no one can call you—to promise his wife repeatedly that once he was released, he would never get into trouble with the law again. Sally was reassured by this news.

In Doug's absence, and despite being heavily pregnant, Sally was still holding down her job at the estate agent's, and had even managed to hire out Doug's lorry for the period of time he would be away. However, Doug wasn't telling his wife the whole story. While other prisoners were being sent in *Playboy*, *Readers' Wives* and the *Sun*, Doug was receiving *Haulage Weekly* and *Exchange & Mart* for his bedside reading.

He was browsing through *Haulage Weekly* when he found exactly what he was looking for: a secondhand, left-hand-drive, forty-ton, American Peterbilt lorry, which was being offered for sale at a knock-down price. Doug took a long time—but then he had a long time—considering the vehicle's added extras. While he sat alone in the library, he began to draw diagrams on the back of the magazine. He then used a ruler to measure the exact size of a box of Marlboro. He realized that the cash return might be smaller this time, but at least he wouldn't be caught.

Among the problems of earning £25,000 a week, and not having to pay tax, is that after being released from prison you are expected to settle for a job that only offers you £25,000 a year before tax; a common enough dilemma for most criminals, especially drug dealers.

With less than a month of his sentence to serve, Doug phoned his wife and asked her to sell his top-of-the-range Mercedes truck, in part exchange for the massive second-hand eighteen-wheel Peterbilt lorry that he'd seen advertised in *Haulage Weekly*.

When Sally first saw the truck, she couldn't understand why her husband wanted to exchange his magnificent vehicle for such a monstrosity. She accepted his explanation that he would be able to drive from Sleaford to Marseilles without having to stop for refuelling.

"But it's a left-hand drive."

"Don't forget," Doug reminded her, "the longest section of the journey is from Calais to Marseilles."

*   *   *

Doug turned out to be a model prisoner, so ended up serving only half of his four-year sentence.

On the day of his release, his wife and eighteen-month-old daughter Kelly were waiting for him at the prison gates. Sally drove them back to Sleaford in her old Vauxhall. On arrival, Doug was pleased to find the secondhand pantechnicon parked in the field next to their little cottage.

"But why haven't you sold my old Merc?" he asked.

"Haven't had a decent offer," Sally admitted, "so I hired it out for another year. At least that way it's showing us a small return." Doug nodded. He was pleased to find that both vehicles were spotless, and after an inspection of the engines, discovered they were also in good nick.

Doug went back to work the following morning. He repeatedly assured Sally that he would never make the same mistake twice. He filled up his lorry with sprouts and peas from a local farmer, before setting out on his journey to Marseilles. He then returned to England with a full load of bananas. A suspicious, recently promoted Mark Cainen regularly pulled Doug over so that he could carry out a spot-check to find out what he was bringing back from Marseilles. But however many crates he prised open, they were always filled with bananas. The officer remained unconvinced, but couldn't work out what Doug was up to.

"Give me a break," said Doug, when Mr. Cainen pulled him over yet again in Dover. "Can't you see that I've turned over a new leaf?" The customs officer didn't give him a break because he was convinced it was a tobacco leaf, even if he couldn't prove it.

Doug's new system was working like a dream, and although he was now only clearing £10,000 a week, at least this time he couldn't be caught. Sally kept all the books up to date for both lorries so that Doug's tax returns were always filled in correctly and paid on time, and any new EU regulations were complied with. However, Doug didn't brief his wife on the details of his new untaxed benefit scheme.

One Thursday afternoon, just after Doug had cleared customs in Dover, he drove into the nearest petrol station to refuel before continuing his journey north to Sleaford. An Audi followed him onto the forecourt, and the driver began to curse about how long he was going to have to wait before the massive pantechnicon would be filled up. To his surprise, the lorry driver only took a couple of minutes before he replaced the nozzle in its holder. As Doug drove out onto the road, the car behind moved up to take his place. When Mr. Cainen saw the name on the side of the lorry, his curiosity was aroused. He checked the pump, to find that Doug had only spent £33. He stared at the massive eighteen-wheeler as it trundled off down the highway, aware that with that amount of petrol Doug could only hope to cover a few more miles before he would have to fill up again.

It took Mr. Cainen only a few minutes to catch up with Doug's truck. He then followed the lorry at a safe distance for the next twenty miles before Doug pulled into another petrol station. Once Doug was back on the road a few minutes later, Mr. Cainen checked the pump—£34—only enough to cover another twenty miles. As Doug continued on his journey to Sleaford, the officer returned to Dover with a smile on his face.

When Doug was driving back from Marseilles the following week, he showed no concern when Mr. Cainen asked him to pull over and park his lorry in the customs shed. He knew that every crate on board was, as the manifest stated, full of bananas. However, the customs officer didn't ask Doug to unlock the back door of the truck. He simply walked around the outside of the vehicle clutching a spanner as if it were a tuning fork while he tapped the massive fuel tanks. The officer was not surprised that the eighth tank rang out with a completely different timbre to the other seven. Doug sat around for hours while customs mechanics removed all eight fuel tanks from both sides of the lorry. Only one was half full of diesel, while the other seven contained over £100,000 worth of cigarettes.

On this occasion the judge was less lenient, and Doug was sent down for six years, even after his barrister pleaded that a second child was on the way.

Sally was horrified to discover that Doug had broken his word, and skeptical when he promised her never, ever, again. The moment her husband was locked up, she rented out the second vehicle and returned to her job as an estate agent.

*   *   *

A year later Sally was able to declare an increased income of just over £3,000, on top of her earnings as an estate agent.

Sally's accountant advised her to buy the field next door to the cottage, where the lorries were always parked at night, as she could claim it against tax. "A carpark," he explained, "would be a legitimate business expense."

As Doug had just begun a six-year sentence and was back to earning £12.50 a week as the prison librarian, he was hardly in a position to offer an opinion. However, even he was impressed when, the following year, Sally declared an income of £37,000, which included her added sales bonuses. This time, the accountant advised her to purchase a third lorry.

Doug was eventually released from prison having only served half his sentence (three years). Sally was parked outside the prison gates in her Vauxhall, waiting to drive her husband home. His nine-year- old daughter, Kelly, was strapped into the back, next to her three-year-old sister Sam. Sally had not allowed either of the children to visit their father in prison, so when Doug took the little girl in his arms for the first time, Sam burst into tears. Sally explained to her that the strange man was her father.

Over a welcome breakfast of bacon and eggs, Sally was able to report that she had been advised by her accountant to form a limited company. Haslett Haulage had declared a profit of £21,600 in its first year, and she had added two more lorries to their growing fleet. Sally told her husband that she was thinking of giving up her job at the estate agent's to become full-time chair of the new company.

"Chair?" said Doug. "What's that?"

Doug was only too pleased to leave Sally to run the company, as long as he was allowed to take his place behind the wheel as one of her drivers. This state of affairs would have continued quite happily, if Doug had not once again been approached by the man from Marseilles—who never seemed to end up in jail—with what he confidently assured him was a fool-proof plan with no risks attached and, more important, this time his wife need never find out.

Doug resisted the Frenchman's advances for several months, but after losing a rather

large sum in a poker game, finally suc-
cumbed. Just one trip, he promised himself.
The man from Marseilles smiled, as he
handed over an envelope containing £12,500
in cash.

Under Sally's chairmanship, the Haslett Haulage Company continued to grow, in both reputation and below the bottom line. Meanwhile, Doug once again became used to having cash in hand; money which did not rely on a balance sheet, and was not subject to a tax return.

Someone else was continuing to keep a close eye on the Haslett Haulage Company, and Doug in particular. Regular as clockwork, Doug could be seen driving his lorry through the Dover terminal, with a full load of sprouts and peas, destined for Marseilles. But Mark Cainen, now an anti-smuggling officer working as part of the Law Enforcement Unit, never once saw Doug make the return journey. This worried him.

The officer checked his records, to find that Haslett Haulage was now running nine lorries a week to different parts of Europe. Their chairman, Sally Haslett, had a spotless reputation—not unlike her vehicles—with everyone she dealt with, from customs to customers. But Mr. Cainen was still curious to find out why Doug was no longer driving back through his port. He took it personally.

A few discreet inquiries revealed that Doug could still be seen in Marseilles unloading his sprouts and peas, and later loading up with crates of bananas. However, there was one slight variation. He was now driving back via Newhaven, which Cainen estimated must have added at least a couple of hours to Doug's journey.

All customs officers have the option of serving one month a year at another port of entry, to further their promotion prospects. The previous year Mr. Cainen had selected Heathrow airport; that year he opted for a month in Newhaven.

Officer Cainen waited patiently for Doug's lorry to appear on the dockside, but it wasn't until the end of his second week that he spotted his old adversary waiting in line to disembark from an Olsen's ferry. The moment Doug's lorry drove onto the dock, Mr. Cainen disappeared upstairs into the staffroom and poured himself a cup of coffee. He walked across to the window and watched Doug's vehicle come to a halt at the front of the line. He was waved quickly through by the two officers on duty. Mr. Cainen made no attempt to intervene as Doug drove out onto the road to continue his journey back to Sleaford. He had to wait another ten days before Doug's lorry reappeared, and this time he noted that only one thing hadn't changed. Mr. Cainen didn't think it was a coincidence.

When Doug returned via Newhaven five days later, the same two officers gave his vehicle no more than a cursory glance, before waving him through. The officer now knew that it wasn't a coincidence. Mr. Cainen reported his observations to his boss in Newhaven and, as his month was up, made his way back to Dover.

Doug completed three more journeys from Marseilles via Newhaven before the two customs officers were arrested. When Doug saw five officers heading toward his truck, he knew that his new impossible-to-be-caught system had been sussed.

Doug didn't waste the court's time pleading not guilty, because one of the customs officers with whom he had been splitting the take had made a deal to have his sentence reduced if he named names. He named Douglas Arthur Haslett.

The judge sent Doug down for eight years, with no remission for good behavior, unless he agreed to pay a fine of £750,000. Doug didn't have £750,000 and begged Sally to help out, as he couldn't face the thought of another eight years behind bars. Sally had to sell everything, including the cottage, the carpark, nine lorries and even her engagement ring, so that her husband could comply with the court order.

After serving a year at Wayland Category C prison in Norfolk, Doug was transferred back to North Sea Camp. Once again, he was appointed as librarian, which was where I first met him.

I was impressed that Sally and his two— now grown-up—daughters came to visit Doug every weekend. He told me that they didn't discuss business, even though he'd sworn on his mother's grave never, ever again.

"Don't even think about it," Sally had warned him. "I've already sent your lorry to the scrapyard."

"Can't blame the woman, after all I've put her through," said Doug when I next visited the library. "But if they won't let me get behind a wheel once I'm released, what am I going to do for the rest of my life?"

*   *   *

I was released a couple of years before Doug, and if I hadn't been addressing a literary festival in Lincoln some years later, I might never have discovered what had become of the chief librarian.

As I stared down into the audience during questions, I thought I recognized three vaguely familiar faces looking up at me from the third row. I racked that part of my brain that is meant to store names, but it didn't respond. That was, until I had a question about the difficulties of writing while in prison. Then it all came flooding back. I had last seen Sally some three years before, when she was visiting Doug accompanied by her two daughters, Kelly and, and . . . Sam.

After I'd taken the final question, we broke for coffee, and the three of them came across to join me.

"Hi, Sally. How's Doug?" I asked even before they could introduce themselves. An old political ploy, and they looked suitably impressed.

"Retired," said Sally without explanation.

"But he was younger than me," I protested, "and never stopped telling every-

one what he planned to do once he was released."

"No doubt," said Sally, "but I can assure
you he's retired. Haslett Haulage is now run
by me and my two daughters, with a back-
room staff of twenty-one, not including the
drivers."

"So you're obviously doing well," I said,
fishing.

"You clearly don't read the financial
pages," she teased.

"I'm like the Japanese," I countered, "I always read my papers from back to front. So
what have I missed?"

"We went public last year," chipped in
Kelly. "Mum's chair, I'm in charge of new accounts and Sam is responsible for the drivers."

"And if I remember correctly, you had
about nine lorries?"

"We now have forty-one," said Sally, "and
our turnover last year was just under five
million."

"And Doug doesn't play any role?"

"Doug plays golf," said Sally, "which
doesn't require him to travel through Dover,
or," she added with a sigh, as her husband

appeared in the doorway, "back via Newhaven."

Doug remained still, as his eyes searched the room for his family. I waved and caught his attention. Doug waved back and wandered slowly across to join us.

"We still allow him to drive us home from time to time," whispered Sam with a grin, just as Doug appeared by my side.

I shook hands with my former inmate, and when Sally and the girls had finished their coffee, I accompanied them all back to their car, which gave me the chance to have a word with Doug.

"I'm delighted to hear that Haslett Haulage is doing so well," I volunteered.

"Put it all down to experience," said Doug. "Don't forget I taught them everything they know."

"And since we last met, Kelly tells me that the company's gone public."

"All part of my long-term plan," said Doug as his wife climbed into the back of the car. He turned and gave me a knowing look. "A lot of people sniffing around at the moment, Jeff, so don't be surprised if there's a takeover bid in the near future."

Just as he reached the driver's side of the car, he added, "Chance for you to make a few bob while the shares are still at their present price. Know what I mean?"

Charity Begins at Home

Henry Preston, Harry to his friends—and they didn't number many—wasn't the sort of person you'd bump into at the local pub, meet at a football match or invite home for a barbecue. Frankly, if there was a club for introverts, Henry would be elected chairman—reluctantly.

At school, the only subject in which he excelled was mathematics, and his mother, the one person who adored him, was determined that Henry would have a profession. His father had been a postman. With one A level in maths, the field was fairly limited—

banking or accountancy. His mother chose accountancy.

Henry was articled to Pearson, Clutterbuck & Reynolds, and when he first joined the firm as a clerk he dreamed of the headed notepaper reading *Pearson, Clutterbuck, Reynolds & Preston*. But as the years went by, and younger and younger men found their names embossed on the left-hand side of the company notepaper, the dream faded.

Some men, aware of their limitations, find solace in another form—sex, drugs or a hectic social life. It's quite difficult to conduct a hectic social life on your own. Drugs? Henry didn't even smoke, although he allowed himself the occasional gin and tonic, but only on Saturday. And as for sex, he felt confident he wasn't gay, but his success rate with the opposite sex, "hits" as some of his younger colleagues described them, hovered around zero. Henry didn't even have a hobby.

There comes a point in every man's life when he realizes *I'm going to live forever* is a fallacy. It came all too soon for Henry, as he progressed quickly through middle age and suddenly began to think about early retirement. When Mr. Pearson, the senior partner, retired, a large party was held in his honor in a private room at a five-star hotel. Mr. Pearson, after a long and distinguished career, told his colleagues that he would be retiring to a cottage in the Cotswolds to tend the roses and try to lower his golf handicap. Much laughter and applause followed. The only thing Henry recalled of that occasion was Atkins, the firm's latest recruit, saying to him as he left for the evening, "I suppose it won't be that long, old chap, before we're doing the same sort of thing for you."

Henry mulled over young Atkins's words as he walked toward the bus stop. He was fifty-four years old, so in six years' time, unless he made partner, in which case his tenure would be extended to sixty-five, they would be holding a farewell party for him. In truth, Henry had long ago given up any thought of becoming a partner, and he had already accepted that his party would not be held in the private room of a five-star hotel. He certainly wouldn't be retiring to a cottage in the Cotswolds to tend his roses, and he already had enough handicaps, without thinking about golf.

Henry was well aware that his colleagues considered him to be reliable, competent and thorough, which only added to his sense of failure. The highest praise he ever received was, "You can always depend on Henry. He's a safe pair of hands."

But all of that changed the day he met Angela.

Angela Forster's company, Events Unlimited, was neither large enough to be assigned to one of the partners, nor small enough to be handled by an articled clerk, which is how her file ended up on Henry's desk. He studied the details carefully.

Ms. Forster was the sole proprietor of a small business that specialized in organizing events—anything from the local Conservative Association's annual dinner to a regional Hunt Ball. Angela was a born organizer and after her husband left her for a younger woman—when a man leaves his wife for a younger woman, it's a short story, when a woman leaves her husband for a younger man, it's a novel (I digress)—Angela made the decision not to sit at home and feel sorry for herself but, following our Lord's advice in the parable of the talents, opted to use her one gift, so that she could fully occupy her time while making a little pin money on the side. The problem was that Angela had become a little more successful than she'd anticipated, which is how she ended up having an appointment with Henry.

Before Henry finalized Ms. Forster's accounts, he took her slowly through the figures, column by column, showing his new client how she was entitled to claim for certain items against tax, such as her car, travel and even her clothes. He pointed out that she ought to be dressed appropriately when she attended one of her functions. Henry managed to save Ms. Forster a few hundred pounds on her tax bill; after all, he considered it a matter of professional pride that, having heeded his advice, all his clients left the office better off. That was even after they'd settled his company's fees, which, he pointed out, could also be claimed against tax.

Henry always ended every meeting with the words, "I can assure you that your accounts are in apple-pie order, and the tax man will not be troubling you." Henry was only too aware that very few of his clients were likely to interest the tax man, let alone be troubled by him. He would then accompany his client to the door with the words, "See you next year." When he opened the door for Ms. Forster, she smiled, and said, "Why don't you come along to one of my functions, Mr. Preston? Then you can see what I get up to most evenings."

Henry couldn't recall when he'd last been invited to anything. He hesitated, not quite sure how to respond. Angela filled the silence. "I'm organizing a ball for African famine relief on Saturday evening. It's at the town hall. Why don't you join me?"

Henry heard himself saying, "Yes, thank you, how nice. I'll look forward to it," and regretted the decision the moment he had closed the door. After all, on Saturday nights he always watched film of the week on Sky, while enjoying a Chinese takeaway and a gin and tonic. In any case, he needed to be in bed by ten because on Sunday morning he was responsible for checking the church collection. He was also their accountant. Honorary, he assured his mother.

Henry spent most of Saturday morning trying to come up with an excuse: a headache, an emergency meeting, a previous engagement he'd forgotten about, so that he could ring Ms. Forster and call the whole thing off. Then he realized that he didn't have her home number.

At six o'clock that evening Henry put on the dinner jacket his mother had given him on his twenty-first birthday, which didn't always have an annual outing. He looked at himself in the mirror, nervous that his attire must surely be out of date—wide lapels and flared trousers—unaware that this look was actually back in fashion. He was among the last to arrive at the town hall, and had already made up his mind that he would be among the first to leave.

Angela had placed Henry on the end of the top table, from where he was able to observe proceedings, while only occasionally having to respond to the lady seated on his left.

Once the speeches were over, and the band had struck up, Henry felt he could safely slip away. He looked around for Ms. Forster. He had earlier spotted her dashing all over the place, organizing everything from the raffle and the heads-and-tails competition to the ten-pound-note draw and even the auction. When he looked at her more closely, dressed in her long red ball gown, her fair hair falling to her shoulders, he had to admit . . . Henry stood up and was about to leave, when Angela appeared by his side. "Hope you've enjoyed yourself," she said, touching his arm. Henry couldn't remember the last time a woman had touched him. He prayed she wasn't going to ask him to dance.

"I've had a wonderful time," Henry assured her. "How about you?"

"Run off my feet," Angela replied, "but I

feel confident that we'll raise a record amount this year."

"So how much do you expect to make?" asked Henry, relieved to find himself on safer ground.

Angela checked her little notebook. "Twelve thousand, six hundred in pledges, thirty-nine thousand, four hundred and fifty in checks, and just over twenty thousand in cash." She handed over her notebook for Henry to inspect. He expertly ran a finger down the list of figures, relaxing for the first time that evening.

"What do you do with the cash?" Henry asked.

"I always drop it off on my way home at the nearest bank that has an overnight safe. If you'd like to accompany me, you'll have experienced the whole cycle from beginning to end." Henry nodded.

"Just give me a few minutes," she said. "I have to pay the band, as well as my helpers—and they always insist on cash."

That was probably when Henry first had the idea. Just a passing thought to begin with, which he quickly dismissed. He headed toward the exit and waited for Angela.

"If I remember correctly," said Henry as they walked down the steps of the town hall together, "your turnover last year was just under five million, of which over a million was in cash."

"What a good memory you have, Mr. Preston," Angela said as they headed toward the High Street, "but I'm hoping to raise over five million this year," she added, "and I'm already ahead of my target for March."

"That may well be the case," said Henry, "but you still only paid yourself forty-two thousand last year," he continued, "which is less than one percent of your turnover."

"I'm sure you're right," said Angela, "but I enjoy the work, and it keeps me occupied."

"But don't you consider you deserve a better return for your efforts?"

"Possibly, but I only charge my clients five percent of the profits, and every time I suggest putting my fee up, they always remind me that they are a charity."

"But you're not," said Henry. "You're a professional, and should be recompensed accordingly."

"I know you're right," said Angela as they stopped outside the Nat West bank and she dropped the cash into the night safe, "but most of my clients have been with me for years."

"And have taken advantage of you for years," insisted Henry.

"That may well be so," said Angela, "but what can I do about it?"

The thought returned to Henry's mind, but he said nothing other than, "Thank you for a most interesting evening, Ms. Forster. I haven't enjoyed myself so much in years." Henry thrust out his right hand, as he always did at the end of every meeting, and had to stop himself saying, "See you next year."

Angela laughed, leaned forward and kissed him on the cheek. Henry certainly couldn't remember when that had last occurred. "Goodnight, Henry," she said as she turned and began to walk away.

"I don't suppose . . ." he hesitated.

"Yes, Henry?" she said, turning back to face him.

"That you'd consider having dinner with me some time?"

"I'd like that very much," said Angela. "When would suit you?"

"Tomorrow," said Henry, suddenly emboldened.

Angela removed a diary from her handbag and began to flick through the pages. "I know I can't do tomorrow," she said. "I have a feeling it's Greenpeace."

"Monday?" said Henry, not having to check his diary.

"Sorry, it's the Blue Cross Ball," said Angela, turning another page of her diary.

"Tuesday?" said Henry trying not to sound desperate.

"Amnesty International," said Angela, flicking over another page.

"Wednesday," said Henry, wondering if she had changed her mind.

"Looks good," said Angela, staring at a blank page. "Where would you like to meet?"

"How about La Bacha?" said Henry, remembering that it was the restaurant where the partners always took their most important clients to lunch. "Eight o'clock suit you?"

"Suits me fine."

Henry arrived at the restaurant twenty minutes early and read the menu from cover to cover—several times. During his lunch break, he'd purchased a new shirt and a silk tie. He was already regretting that he hadn't tried on the blazer that was displayed in the window.

Angela strolled into La Bacha just after eight. She was wearing a pale green floral dress that fell just below the knee. Henry liked the way she'd done her hair, but knew that he wouldn't have the courage to tell her. He also approved of the fact that she wore so little make-up and her only jewelry was a modest string of pearls. Henry rose from his place as she reached the table. Angela couldn't remember the last person who'd bothered to do that.

Henry had feared that they wouldn't be able to find anything to talk about—small talk had never been his forte—but Angela made it all so easy that he found himself ordering a second bottle of wine, long before the meal was over—another first.

Over coffee, Henry said, "I think I've come up with a way of supplementing your income."

"Oh, don't let's talk business," said Angela, touching his hand.

"It's not business," Henry assured her.

When Angela woke the following morning, she smiled as she remembered what a pleasant evening she'd spent with Henry. All she could recall him saying as they parted was, "Don't forget that any winnings made from gambling are tax-free." What was all that about?

Henry, on the other hand, could recall every detail of the advice he'd given Angela. He rose early on the following Sunday and began preparing an outline plan, which included opening several bank accounts, preparing spreadsheets and working on a long-term investment program. He nearly missed matins.

The following evening Henry made his way to the Hilton Hotel on Park Lane, arriving a few minutes after midnight. He was carrying an empty Gladstone bag in one hand and an umbrella in the other. After all, he had to look the part.

The Westminster and City Conservative Association's annual ball was coming to an end. As Henry entered the ballroom, party-goers were beginning to burst balloons and drain the last drops of champagne from any remaining bottles. He spotted Angela seated at a table in the far corner, sorting out pledges, checks and cash before placing them in three separate piles. She looked up and couldn't mask her surprise when she saw him. Angela had spent the day convincing herself that he didn't mean it and, if he did turn up, she wouldn't go through with it.

"How much cash?" he asked matter-of-factly, even before she could say hello.

"Twenty-two thousand three hundred and seventy pounds," she heard herself saying.

Henry took his time. He double-checked the notes before placing the cash in his battered bag. Angela's calculation had proved to be accurate. He handed her a receipt for £19,400.

"See you later," he said, just as the band struck up "Jerusalem." Henry left the ballroom as the words "Bring me my bow of burning gold" were rendered lustily and out of tune. Angela remained transfixed as she watched Henry walk away. She knew that if she didn't chase after him and stop the man before he reached the bank, there could be no turning back.

"Congratulations on another well-organized event, Angela," said Councillor Pickering, interrupting her thoughts. "I don't know how we'd manage without you."

"Thank you," said Angela, turning to face the chairman of the ball committee.

Henry pushed his way through the hotel's swing doors and out onto the street, feeling for the first time that his anonymity was no longer a weakness but a strength. He could hear his heart beating as he headed toward the local branch of HSBC, the nearest bank with an overnight safe deposit. Henry dropped £19,400 into the safe, leaving £2,970 of the cash in his bag. He then hailed a taxi—another departure from his usual routine—and gave the cabby an address in the West End.

The taxi drew up outside an establishment that Henry had never entered before, although he had kept their accounts for over twenty years.

The night manager of the Black Ace Casino tried not to look surprised when Mr. Preston walked onto the floor. Had he come to make a spot-check? It seemed unlikely, as the company accountant didn't acknowledge him but headed straight for the roulette table.

Henry knew the odds only too well because he signed off the casino's end-of-year balance sheet every April, and despite rent, rates, staff wages, security and even free meals and drinks for favored customers, his client still managed to declare a handsome profit. But it wasn't Henry's intention to make a profit, or, for that matter, a loss.

Henry took a seat at the roulette table and saw red. He opened his Gladstone bag, extracted ten ten-pound notes and handed them across to the croupier, who in turn counted them slowly before he gave Henry ten little blue and white chips in return.

There were a number of gamblers already seated at the table, placing bets of different denominations, five, ten, twenty, fifty and even the occasional hundred-pound golden chip. Only one punter had a stack of golden chips in front of him, which he was spreading randomly around the different numbers. Henry was pleased to see that he held the attention of most of the onlookers standing round the table.

While the man on the far side of the table continued to litter the green baize with golden chips, Henry placed one of his ten-pound chips on red. The wheel spun and the little white ball revolved in the opposite direction until it finally settled in red 19. The croupier returned one ten-pound chip to Henry, while he raked in over a thousand pounds' worth of golden chips from the gambler on the other side of the table.

While the croupier prepared for the next spin of the wheel, Henry slipped his single chip in the left-hand pocket of his jacket, while leaving his original stake on red.

The croupier spun the wheel again and this time the little white ball came to a halt in black 4, and Henry's chip was raked in by the croupier. Two bets, and Henry had bro-

ken even. He placed another ten-pound chip on red. Henry had already accepted that if he was to exchange all the cash for chips, it would be a long and arduous process. But then Henry, unlike most gamblers, was a patient man, whose only purpose was to break even. He placed another ten pounds on red.

Three hours later, by which time he had managed to exchange all £2,970 of cash for chips without anyone becoming suspicious, Henry left the table and headed for the bar. If any one had been following closely what Henry had been up to, they would have observed that he had just about broken even. But then that was his intention. He only ever meant to exchange all the surplus cash for chips before he could execute the second part of his plan.

When Henry reached the bar, his Gladstone bag empty and his pockets bulging with chips, he took a seat next to a woman who appeared to be on her own. He didn't speak to her and she showed no interest in him. When Angela ordered another drink, Henry bent down and deposited all of his chips into the open handbag she had left on the floor beside her. He was already walking toward the exit before the barman could take his order.

The manager pulled open the front door for him.

"I hope it won't be too long before we see you again, sir."

Henry nodded, but didn't bother to explain that the whole exercise was about to

become part of a nightly routine. Once
Henry was back outside on the pavement,
he walked toward the nearest tube station,
but didn't start whistling until he'd turned
the corner.

Angela bent down and closed her bag,
but not before she'd finished her drink. Two
men had propositioned her earlier in the
evening and she'd felt quite flattered. She
slipped off her stool and walked across to
join a short queue of punters at the cashier's
window. When she reached the front, Angela pushed the pile of ten-pound chips under the steel grille and waited.

"Cash or check, madam?" inquired the
teller, once he'd counted her chips.

"A check please," Angela replied.

"What name should the check be made
out to?" was the teller's next question.

After a moment's hesitation, Angela said,
"Mrs. Ruth Richards."

The cashier wrote out the name Ruth
Richards, and the figure, £2,930, before
slipping the check under the grille. Angela
checked the figure. Henry had lost £40. She
smiled, remembering that he had assured
her that over a year it would even out. After
all, as he had explained often enough, he

wasn't playing the odds, but simply ex-
changing any traceable cash for chips, so
that she would end up with a check which
no one would later be able to trace.

Angela slipped out of the casino when
she saw the manager chatting to another
customer who had clearly lost a large sum
of money. Henry had warned her that the
management keeps a much closer eye on
winners than losers, and that as she was
about to embark on a long and profitable
run she shouldn't draw attention to herself.

One of Henry's stipulations was that
there should not be any contact between
the two of them, other than when he came
to collect the takings, and then again for
that brief moment when he deposited the
chips into her open bag. He didn't want
anyone to think that they might be an item.
Angela reluctantly agreed with his reason-
ing. Henry's only other piece of advice was
that she should not be seen collecting the
cash herself during any function.

"Leave that to the volunteers," he said,
"so that if anything goes wrong, no one will
suspect you."

There are one hundred and twelve casinos located across central London, so

Henry and Angela didn't find it necessary to return to any particular establishment more than once a year.

For the next three years, Henry and Angela took their holidays at the same time, but never in the same place, and always in August. Angela explained that not many organizations hold their annual events in that particular month. During the season Henry had to make sure that he was never out of town because from September to December Sunday was the only night Angela could guarantee not to be working, and in the run-up to Christmas she often had a lunchtime event, followed by a couple more functions in the evening.

Although Henry had written the rulebook, Angela had insisted on adding a subclause. Nothing would be deducted from any organization which failed to reach the previous year's total. Despite this addendum, which incidentally Henry heartily agreed with, he rarely left a function with his Gladstone bag empty.

The two of them still met once a year at Mr. Preston's office to go over Ms. Forster's an-

nual accounts, which was followed by a
dinner a week later at La Bacha. Neither of
them ever alluded to the fact that she had
siphoned off £267,900, £311,150 and
£364,610 during the past three years, and
after each function deposited the latest
check in different bank accounts right
across London, always in the name of Mrs.
Ruth Richards. Henry's other responsibility
was to ensure that their new-found wealth
was invested shrewdly, remembering that
he wasn't a gambler. However, one of the
advantages of preparing other companies'
accounts is that it isn't too difficult to predict who is likely to have a good year. As the
checks were never made out in his or her
name, any subsequent profits couldn't be
traced back to either of them.

After they had banked the first million,
Henry felt that they could risk a celebration
dinner. Angela wanted to go to Mosimann's
in West Halkin Street, but Henry vetoed the
idea. He booked a table for two at La
Bacha. No need to draw attention to their
new-found wealth, he reminded her.

Henry made two other suggestions during dinner. Angela was quite happy to go
along with the first, but didn't want to talk

about the second. Henry had advised her to transfer the first million to an offshore account in the Cook Islands, while he carried on with the same investment policy; he also recommended that in future whenever they cleared another hundred thousand, Angela would immediately transfer the sum to the same account.

Angela raised her glass. "Agreed," she said, "but what is the second item on the agenda, Mr. Chairman?" she asked, teasing him. Henry took her through the details of a contingency plan she didn't even want to think about.

Henry finally raised his glass. For the first time in his life, he was looking forward to retirement, and joining all his colleagues for a farewell party on his sixtieth birthday.

Six months later, the chairman of Pearson, Clutterbuck & Reynolds sent out invitations to all the firm's employees, asking them to join the partners for drinks at a local three-star hotel to celebrate the retirement of Henry Preston and to thank him for forty years of dedicated service to the company.

Henry was unable to attend his own farewell party, as he ended up celebrating his sixtieth birthday behind bars, and all for a mere £820.

Miss Florence Blenkinsopp double-checked the figures. She'd been right the first time. They were £820 short of the amount she had calculated before the uninvited guest dressed in a pinstriped suit had walked into the ballroom with his little bag and disappeared with all the cash. It couldn't be Angela who was responsible; after all, she had been one of her pupils at St. Catherine's Convent. Miss Blenkinsopp dismissed the discrepancy as her mistake, especially as the takings were comfortably up on the previous year's total.

The following year would be the convent's one-hundredth anniversary, and Miss Blenkinsopp was already planning a centenary ball. She told her committee that she expected them to pull their socks up if they hoped to set records during the centenary year. Although Miss Blenkinsopp had retired as headmistress of St. Catherine's some seven years before, she continued to treat her committee of old gals as if they were still adolescent pupils.

The centenary ball could not have been a greater success, and Miss Blenkinsopp was the first to single out Angela for particular praise. She made it clear that in her opinion, Ms. Forster had certainly pulled her socks up. However, Miss Blenkinsopp felt it necessary to triple-check the cash they had collected that night, before the little man turned up with his Gladstone bag and took it all away. When she went over the figures later in the week, although their previous record had been broken by a considerable amount, the cash entry was over two thousand short of the figure she had scribbled on the back of her place card.

Miss Blenkinsopp felt she had no choice but to point out the discrepancy (two years running) to her president, Lady Travington, who in turn sought the advice of her husband, who was chairman of the local watch committee. Sir David promised, before putting the light out that night, that he would have a word with the chief constable in the morning.

When the chief constable was informed of the misappropriation, he passed on the details to his chief superintendent. He sent it further down the line to a chief inspector, who would like to have told his boss that he was in the middle of a murder hunt and also staking out a shipment of heroin with a street value of over ten million. The fact that St. Catherine's Convent had mislaid—he checked his notes—just over £2,000, wasn't likely to be placed at the top of his priority list. He stopped the next person walking down the corridor and passed her the file. "See you have a full report on my desk, Sergeant, before the watch committee meet next month."

Detective Sergeant Janet Seaton set about her task as if she was stalking Jack the Ripper.

First, she interviewed Miss Blenkinsopp, who was most cooperative, but insisted that none of her gals could possibly have been involved with such an unpleasant incident, and therefore they were not to be interviewed. Ten days later, DS Seaton purchased a ticket for the Bebbington Hunt Ball, despite the fact that she had never mounted a horse in her life.

DS Seaton arrived at Bebbington Hall just

before the gong was struck and the toast-master bellowed out, "Dinner is served." She quickly identified Angela Forster, even before she had located her table. Although DS Seaton had to engage in polite conversation with the men on either side of her, she was still able to keep a roving eye on Ms. Forster. By the time cheese and coffee were served, the detective had come to the conclusion that she was dealing with a consummate professional. Not only could Ms. Forster handle the regular outbursts of Lady Bebbington, the Master of Hounds' wife, but she also found time to organize the band, the kitchen, the waiters, the cabaret and the voluntary staff without once breaking into a gallop. But, more interesting, she seemed to have nothing to do with the collecting of any money. That was carried out by a group of ladies, who performed the task without appearing to consult Angela.

When the band struck up its opening number, several young men asked the detective sergeant for a dance. She turned them all down, one somewhat reluctantly.

It was a few minutes before one, when the evening was drawing to a close, that the detective sergeant spotted the man she had been waiting for. Among the red and black jackets, he would have been easier to identify than a fox on the run. He also fitted the exact description Miss Blenkinsopp had provided: a short, rotund, bald-headed man of around sixty who would be more appropriately dressed for an accountant's office than a Hunt Ball. She never took her eyes off him as he progressed unobtrusively around the outside of the dance floor to disappear behind the bandstand. The detective quickly left her table and walked to the other side of the ballroom, coming to a halt only when she had a perfect sighting of the two of them. The man was seated next to Angela counting the cash, unaware that an extra pair of eyes was watching him. The detective sergeant stared at Angela, as the man carefully placed the checks, the pledges and the cash in separate piles. Not a word passed between them.

Once Henry had double-checked the amount of cash, he didn't even give Angela a second look. He placed the notes in his bag and handed her a receipt. With no more than a slight bow of the head, he retraced his steps round the outside of the dance floor and quickly left the ballroom. The whole operation had taken him less than seven minutes. Henry didn't notice that one of the revellers was only a few paces behind him, and, more important, her eyes never left him.

DS Seaton watched as the unidentified man made his way down the long drive, through the wrought-iron gates and on toward the village.

Since it was a clear night and the streets were empty, it was not difficult for DS Seaton to follow the progress of the man with the bag without being spotted. He must have been supremely confident because he never once looked back. She only had to slip into the shadows on one occasion, when her quarry came to a halt outside a local branch of the Nat West Bank. He opened his bag, removed a package and dropped it into the overnight safe. He then continued on his way, hardly breaking his stride. Where was he going?

The young detective had to make an instant decision. Should she follow the stranger, or return to Bebbington Hall and see what Ms. Forster was up to? Follow the money, she had always been instructed by her supervisor at Peel House. When Henry reached the station, the detective sergeant cursed. She had left her car in the grounds of the hall, and if she was to continue pursuing the bag man, she would have to abandon the vehicle and pick it up first thing in the morning.

The last train to Waterloo that night trundled into Bebbington Halt a few minutes later. It was becoming clear that the man with the bag had everything timed to the minute. The detective remained out of sight until her suspect had boarded the train. She then took a seat in the next carriage.

When they reached Waterloo, the man stepped off the train and made his way quickly across to the nearest taxi rank. The detective stood to one side and watched as he progressed to the front of the queue. The moment he climbed into a cab, the detective walked briskly to the top of the queue, produced her warrant card and apologized to the person who was about to step into a cab. She jumped in the taxi and instructed the driver to follow the one that had just moved off the rank.

When the driver pulled up outside the Black Ace Casino, the detective remained in

the back of her cab until the man had disappeared inside.

She took her time paying the cab driver
before she climbed out and followed her
quarry into the casino. She filled in a temporary membership form, as she didn't want
anyone to realize that she was on duty.

DS Seaton strolled onto the floor and
glanced around the gaming tables. It only
took her a few moments before she spotted
her man seated next to one of the roulette
wheels. She took a step closer and joined a
group of onlookers who formed a horse-
shoe around the table. The detective sergeant made sure that she remained some
distance away from her quarry because,
dressed in a long blue silk gown more appropriate for a ball, he might spot her and
even wonder if she had followed him from
Bebbington Hall.

For the next hour she watched the man
remove wads of cash from his bag at regular intervals, then exchange them for chips.
An hour later the bag was clearly empty because he left the table with a glum look on
his face, and made his way toward the bar.

DS Seaton had cracked it. The anonymous man was siphoning off money from the evening events in order to finance his gambling habit, but she still couldn't be sure if Angela was involved.

The detective slipped behind a marble pillar as the man climbed onto a stool next to a lady in a blue suit with a short skirt.

Did he have enough money over to pay for a prostitute? The detective stepped out from behind the pillar to take a closer look, and nearly bumped into Henry as he began walking back toward the exit. Later, much later, DS Seaton thought it strange that he had left the bar without having a drink. Perhaps the woman on the stool had rejected him.

Henry stepped out onto the pavement and hailed a taxi. The detective grabbed the next one. She followed his cab as it made its way across Putney Bridge and continued its journey along the south side of the river. The taxi finally came to a halt outside a block of flats in Wandsworth. DS Seaton made a note of the address and decided that she had earned a taxi ride home.

The following morning, DS Seaton placed her report on the chief inspector's desk. He read it, smiled, left his office and walked down the corridor to brief the chief superintendent, who in turn phoned the chief constable. The chief decided not to mention it to the chairman of the watch committee until after an arrest had been made, as he wanted to present Sir David with an open-

and-shut case, one that a jury could not fail to convict on.

Henry deposited the cash from the Butterfly Ball in the overnight vault of Lloyds TSB just a couple of hundred yards away from the hotel where the Masons were holding their annual dinner. He must have walked about another thirty yards before a police car drew up beside him. There wouldn't have been much point in making a dash for it, as Henry wasn't built for a change of gear. And in any case he had already planned for this moment, right down to the last detail. Henry was arrested and charged two days before the watch committee was due to meet.

Henry selected Mr. Clifton-Smyth to represent him, a solicitor whose accounts he had handled for the past twenty years.

Mr. Clifton-Smyth listened carefully to his client's defense, making copious notes, but when Henry finally came to the end of his tale, the lawyer only had one piece of advice to offer him: plead guilty.

"I will of course," added the lawyer, "brief counsel of any mitigating circumstances."

Henry accepted his solicitor's advice; after all, Mr. Clifton-Smyth had never once, in the past two decades, questioned *his* judgment.

Henry made no attempt to contact Angela during the run-up to the trial, and although the police felt fairly confident that she was playing Bonnie to his Clyde, they quickly worked out that they shouldn't have arrested him until he'd gone to the casino a second time. Who was the woman seated at the bar? Had she been waiting for him? The Special Crime Unit spent weeks collecting bank stubs from casinos right across London, but they couldn't find a single check made out to a Ms. Angela Forster, and even more puzzling, they didn't come up with one for a Mr. Henry Preston. Did he always lose?

When they checked Angela's events book, they discovered that Henry had always taken responsibility for counting the cash, and signed the receipt. Her bank account was then picked over by a bunch of treasury vultures, and found to be only £11,318 in credit, a sum that had showed very little movement either way for the past five years. When DS Seaton reported back to Miss Blenkinsopp, she seemed quite content to believe that the right man had been apprehended. After all, she told the detective, a St. Catherine's gal couldn't possibly be involved in that sort of thing.

With the murder hunt still in progress, and the drugs stash not yet unearthed, the chief superintendent sent down an instruction to close the St. Catherine's file. They'd made an arrest, and that was all that would matter when they reported their annual crime statistics.

Once the Treasury solicitors had accepted that they couldn't trace any of the missing money, Henry's solicitor managed to broker a deal with the CPS. If he pleaded guilty to the theft of £130,000, and was willing to return the full amount to the injured parties concerned, they would recommend a reduced sentence.

"And no doubt there are mitigating circumstances in this case that you wish to bring to my attention, Mr. Cameron?" suggested the judge as he stared down from the bench at Henry's Silk.

"There most certainly are, m'lord," replied Mr. Alex Cameron QC as he rose slowly from his place. "My client," he began, "makes no secret of his unfortunate addiction to gambling, which has been the cause of his tragic downfall. However," Mr. Cameron continued, "I feel confident that your lordship will take into account that this is my client's first offense, and until this sad lapse of judgment he had been a pillar of the community with an unblemished reputation. Indeed, my client has given years of selfless service to his local church as its honorary treasurer, to which you will recall, m'lord, the vicar bore witness."

Mr. Cameron cleared his throat before continuing. "M'lord, you see before you a broken and penniless man, who has nothing to look forward to except long lonely years of retirement. He has even," added Mr. Cameron, tugging at his lapels, "had to sell his flat in Wandsworth in order to repay his creditors." He paused. "Perhaps you might feel, in the circumstances, m'lord, that my client has suffered quite enough and should therefore be treated leniently." Mr. Cameron smiled hopefully at the judge, and resumed his seat.

The judge looked down at Henry's advocate, and returned his smile. "Not quite enough, Mr. Cameron. Try not to forget that Mr. Preston was a professional man who violated a position of trust. But first let me remind your client," said the judge, turning his attention to Henry, "that gambling is a sickness, and the defendant should seek some help for his malady the moment he is released from prison." Henry braced himself as he waited to learn how long his sentence would be.

The judge paused for what seemed an eternity, as he continued to stare at Henry. "I sentence you to three years," he said, before adding, "take the prisoner down."

Henry was shipped off to Ford open prison. No one noticed him come and no one noticed him go. He led just as anonymous an existence on the inside as he had outside. He received no mail, made no phone calls and entertained no visitors. When they released him eighteen months later, having completed half his sentence, there was no one waiting at the barrier to greet him.

Henry Preston accepted his £45 discharge pay, and was last seen heading toward the local railway station, carrying a

Gladstone bag containing only his personal belongings.

Mr. and Mrs. Graham Richards enjoy a pleasant, if somewhat uneventful retirement on the island of Majorca. They have a small, front-line villa overlooking the Bay of Palma, and both of them are proving to be popular with the local community.

The chairman of the Royal Overseas Club in Palma reported to the AGM that he considered he'd pulled off quite a coup, convincing the former finance director of the Nigerian National Oil Company to become the club's honorary treasurer. Nods, hear-hears and a sprinkling of applause followed. The chairman went on to suggest that the secretary should record a note in the minutes, that since Mr. Richards had taken over the responsibility as treasurer, the club's accounts had been in apple-pie order.

"And by the way," he added, "his wife Ruth has kindly agreed to organize our annual ball."

The Alibi

"He got away with murder, didn't he?" said Mick.

"How did he manage that?" I asked.

"Because if two screws say that's what happened, then that's what happened," said Mick, "and no con will be able to tell you any different. Understood?"

"No, I don't understand," I admitted.

"Then I'll have to explain it to you, won't I?" said Mick. "There's a golden rule among cons—never have sex with a mate's tart while he's banged up. It's all part of the code."

"That might be a bit rough on a young girl

whose boyfriend has just been given a lengthy sentence because then you'd be sentencing her to the same number of years without sex."

"That's not the point," said Mick, "because Pete made it clear to Karen that he'd wait for her."

"But he wasn't going anywhere for the next six years," I suggested.

"You're missing the point, Jeff. It's the code and, to be fair to the tart, by all accounts Karen was as good as gold for the first six months and then she came off the rails. Truth is," said Mick, "Pete's best mate Brian had already had sex with Karen, but that was before she became Pete's girl, on account of the fact that they'd all been at secondary modern together. But that didn't count because Karen stopped whoring around once she'd moved in with Pete. Understood?"

"I think so," I said.

"Mind you, the rule doesn't apply to Pete on account of the fact that he's a man. It's only logic, isn't it, because men are different. We're lions, they're lambs." Lionesses would have seemed more appropriate. However, I confess I didn't voice my opinion at the time. "Still," Mick continued, "the code is clear. You don't have sex with a mate's tart while he's banged up."

I put my pen down and continued to listen to the Gospel according to St. Mick—another burglar who was in and out of prison as if the building had revolving doors. I decided to abandon any attempt to write my daily diary. It was clear Mick was on a roll and nothing was going to stop him—certainly not me. And as the door was locked and I couldn't escape, I decided to take down his words. But first a little background.

Mick Boyle was my cell mate at Lincoln, and serving his ninth sentence during the past seventeen years, all for burglary. "I may be a tea-leaf," he proclaimed, "but I can't be doing with violence. Don't approve," he added, clearly attempting to capture the moral high ground. He told me that he had six children that he knew of, by five different women, but had had little or no contact with any of them since. I must have looked surprised, because he added, "Don't worry yourself, Jeff, they're all taken care of by the Social."

"If you want pussy," Mick continued,

"there's quite enough going spare without having sex with your best mate's tart; after all, most of us are in and out, in and out," he repeated, laughing at his own joke.

Mick's friend Pete Bailey—the hero or the villain in this tale, according to your viewpoint—had been charged with aggravated robbery, which covers a multitude of sins, especially if you ask the court—after you've been found guilty—to take into consideration one hundred and twelve similar offenses.

"Result? Pete gets six years in the slammer." Mick paused to draw breath. "Mind you, he still killed his best mate while he was inside and got away with it, didn't he?"

"Did he?" I asked, showing a little more interest.

"Yeah, he sure did. Mind you, he knew he'd only have to serve three years on account of the fact that he was always on his best behavior, whenever he was inside," said Mick. "Logic, isn't it? So after fifteen months in Wakefield—awful nick—they sent him off to Hollesley Bay open prison in Suffolk, didn't they, to finish off his sentence. Bloody holiday camp. See, the theory is," continued Mick, "an open prison is meant to prepare you for returning to society. Some hope. All Pete did was spend his time in the prison library reading through back copies of *Country Life*, supplied by some do-gooder, so he could work out in advance which houses he was going to rob the moment he got out. Now another rule in an open prison," continued Mick, "is that you're entitled to a visit once a week, not like the once a month you get in closed conditions; that is as long as you're enhanced, and not been put on report for at least a month."

"Enhanced?" I ventured.

"That's when a con's been on good behavior for at least three months. When he's enhanced he gets all sorts of privileges, like more time out of his cell, better job, even more pay in some nicks."

"And how do you get put on report?"

"That's easy enough. Swear at a screw, turn up late for work, fail a drugs test. I was once put on report for nicking an orange from the kitchen. Diabolical liberty."

"So was your friend Pete ever put on report?" I asked.

"Never," Mick replied. "Good as gold, wasn't he, because he wanted a visit from his tart. Well, he does his three months, works in the stores, keeps his nose clean, and bob's your uncle, he's enhanced. Following Saturday his tart turns up at the nick to pay him a visit.

"In open prisons, visits are held in the biggest room available, usually the gym or the canteen. And you have to remember, security isn't like a closed nick, with sniffer dogs and CCTV cameras following your every move, so you can behave natural when you're with your tart." He paused. "Well, within limits. I mean you can't have sex like they do in Swedish prisons. You know—what do they call it?"

"Conjugal visits?"

"Well, whatever, it's sex, and we don't allow it. Mind you, a screw will turn a blind eye—when a con puts his hand up a tart's skirt, but then I remember in one prison—"

"Pete," I reminded him.

"Oh, yeah, Pete. Well, Karen came to visit Pete the following Saturday. All's going well until Pete asks about his best mate, Brian. Karen clams up, doesn't say a word does she, then turns bright red. Pete susses straight away what she's been up to: tart, having it off with his best mate while he's in-

side. She lit his short fuse, didn't she? So Pete jumps up and puts one on her. Karen goes arse over tits, and lands up flat on the floor. The alarm goes off and screws come running through every door. They had to pull him off Karen and drag him away to segregation. Ever been to segregation, Jeff?"

"No, can't say I have."

"Well, don't bother. Diabolical liberty. Bare cell, mattress on the floor, steel basin

screwed into the wall and a steel bog what
don't flush. Next day Pete's put on report,
and comes up in front of the governor, who,
you have to remember, is God Almighty. He
don't need no judge or jury to help him decide if you're guilty—Home Office regulations are quite enough."

"So what happened to Pete?"

"Sent back to closed conditions, wasn't
he? Shipped off to Lincoln prison the same
day, with another three months added to
his sentence. Some cons, when they're
sent back to a closed nick, lose their rag,
start breaking the place up, taking drugs,
setting their cell on fire, so they never get
out. I was banged up with a muppet in
Liverpool once. Started off with a three-
year sentence and he's still there—eleven
years later. Last time he came up in front of
the governor for—"

"Pete," I said, trying not to sound exasperated.

"Oh, yeah, Pete. Well, Pete goes the
other way."

"The other way?"

"Good as gold all the time he's banged
up at Lincoln. Three months later he's back
enhanced, with all his privileges restored.

Gets a job in the kitchen, works like a slave, six months later he puts in a request for a visit and it's granted, with the exception of one Karen Slater. But he never wanted to see that whore again anyway. No, this time Pete applied for a visit from one of his old mates who was on the out at the time. Now this mate confirms that Brian is not only having it off with Karen, but now that Pete's safely banged up in Lincoln she's moved in with him. What a diabolical liberty," said Mick. "Pete's mate even asked if he wanted Brian done over. 'No, don't go down that road,' Pete told him. 'I'll be taking care of him myself, all in good time.' He never went into no detail of what he had in mind, on account of the fact that in the end someone always opens their mouth. Must be the same in politics, Jeff."

"Pete."

"Well, Pete goes on being as good as gold. Cleanest pad, working all hours, never swearing at no screws, never on report. Result? Twelve months later he's back at Hollesley Bay open prison, with only nine months left to serve."

"And once he was back at Hollesley Bay, did he try to contact Karen?"

"No, didn't put in a request for a visit. In fact, never even mentioned her name."

"So what was his game?" I asked, slipping into the prison jargon.

"He only had one game all along, Jeff: he wanted to get himself transferred to the enhancement block, on the other side of the prison, didn't he."

"I've lost you," I admitted.

"All part of his master plan, wasn't it? When you first arrive at Hollesley Bay, which, don't forget, is an open nick, you're allocated a room in one of the two main blocks."

"Are you?"

"Yeah, north and south block. But if you get enhanced—another three more months of behaving like a saint—then they move you across to the enhancement block, which gives you even more privileges."

"Like what?"

"You can have a visit from a mate every Saturday. Pete wasn't interested. You can go home once a month on a Sunday—he's still not interested. You can apply for a job outside of the prison during the week—still no interest, even though it would of given him a chance to pick up an extra bob or two before he's released."

"Then why bother to earn all those privileges if you don't plan to take advantage of them?" I asked.

"Weren't part of Pete's master plan, was it? Trouble with you, Jeff, is that you don't think like a criminal."

"So why was Pete so keen to get himself transferred to the enhancement block?"

"Good question at last, Jeff, but for that you'll need a little background. Pete 'ad already worked out that over on the enhancement block they 'ad five screws on duty during the day, but only two at night, on account of the fact that if a prisoner reaches enhanced status he can be trusted, not to mention how short-staffed the prison service is. And don't forget that, in an open nick, there are no cells, no bars, no keys and no perimeter walls, so anyone can abscond."

"So why don't they?" I asked.

"Because not many cons who've made it to an open prison are that interested in escaping."

"Why not?"

"Logic, isn't it? They're coming to the end of their sentence, and if they're caught, and nine out of ten of the morons are, you're sent straight back to a closed nick, with extra time added to your sentence. So forget it, it's just not worth it. I remember a con called Dale. What a muppet he was. He only had three weeks left to serve, when he—"

"Pete," I tried again.

"You're such an impatient bastard, Jeff, and it's not as if you're going anywhere. So where was I?"

"Only two officers on duty in the enhancement block at night," I said, checking my notes.

"Oh, yeah. But even on the enhancement block you have to report to the front office at seven in the morning, and then again at nine each night. Now Pete, as I told you, 'ad a job in the prison stores, handing out clothes to the new cons, and supplying laundry once a week for the regulars, so the screws always knew where he was, which was also part of Pete's plan. But if he hadn't reported to the front office at seven in the morning and then again at nine at night, he would have been put on report, which would have meant he'd be sent back to north block with all his privileges removed. So Pete never once misses a roll call, his cell was always spick and span, and his light is always out long before eleven."

"All part of Pete's master plan?"

"You catch on fast," said Mick. "But then Pete came up against an obstacle—that the right word, Jeff?" I nodded, not wishing to interrupt his flow. "During the night, one of the screws would walk round the block at one o'clock and then return again at four in the morning, to check that every con was in bed and asleep. All the screw has to do is pull back the curtain on the outside of the door, look through the glass panel and shine his torch on the bed to make sure the con is snoring away. Have I ever told you about the con who was caught in his room, with a—"

"Pete," I said, not even looking up at Mick.

"Pete would lay awake at night until the first screw came round at one o'clock to make sure he was in his room. The screw lifts the curtain, shines the torch on his bed and then disappears. Pete would then go back to sleep, but he always set his alarm for ten to four when he'd carry out the same routine. A different screw always turns up at four to check you're still in bed. It took Pete just over a month to work out that there were two screws, Mr. Chambers and Mr. Davis, who didn't bother to make the nightly rounds and check everyone was in bed. Chambers used to fall asleep and Davis couldn't be dragged away from the TV. After that, all Pete had to do was wait until the two of them were on duty the same night."

With only about six weeks to go before Pete was due to be released, he returned to the enhancement block after work to find that Chambers and Davis were the duty officers that night. When Pete signed the roll-call sheet at nine, Mr. Chambers was already watching a football match on TV, and Mr. Davis had his feet up on the table drinking a coke and reading the sports pages of the *Sun*. Pete went up to his room, watched TV till just after ten, and then turned off his light. He got into bed and pulled the blanket over him, but kept on his tracksuit and trainers. He waited until a few minutes after one before he crept out into the corridor and checked to make sure no one was around—not a sign of Chambers or Davis. He then went to the end of the corridor, opened the fire-escape door, and disappeared down the back stairs, leaving a wedge of paper in the door, before he set off on an eight-mile run into Woodbridge.

No one can be sure when Pete got back that night, but he reported into the office as usual at seven the next morning. Mr. Chambers ticked off his name. When Pete glanced down at the screw's clipboard, all four of his roll-call columns—nine, one, four and seven—had a tick in every box. Pete had breakfast in the canteen before reporting to the stores for work.

"So he got away with it?"

"Not quite," said Mick. "Later that morning the cops turn up in numbers and begin crawling all over the place, but they're only looking for one man. They end up in the stores, arrest Pete and haul him off to Woodbridge nick for questioning. They interrogate him for hours about the deaths of Brian Powell and Karen Slater, both found strangled in their bed. Rumor has it that they were having it off at the time. Pete stuck to the same line: 'Can't have been me, guv. I was banged up in prison at the time. You only have to ask Mr. Chambers and Mr. Davis, the officers who were on duty that night.' The copper in charge of the case visited the enhancement block and checked the roll-call sheet. Brian and the tart were strangled some time between three and five, according to the police doctor, so if Chambers saw Pete asleep in bed at four, he couldn't have been in Woodbridge at the same time, could he? Logic, isn't it?

"An independent inquiry was set up by the Home Office. Chambers and Davis both confirmed that they'd checked every prisoner at one o'clock and then again at four, and on both occasions Pete had been asleep in his room. Several of the other cons were only too happy to appear in front of the inquiry and confirm they'd been woken by the flashlight, when Chambers and Davis did their rounds. This only strengthened Pete's defense. So the inquiry concluded that Pete must have been in his bed at one o'clock and four o'clock on the night in question, so he couldn't have committed the murders."

"So he got away with it," I repeated.

"Depends on how you describe got away with it," said Mick, "because although the police never charged Pete, the copper in charge of the case later made a statement saying that they'd closed their inquiries, as there was no one else they wanted to interview—hint, hint. That wasn't what you call a good career move for Chambers and Davis, so they set about stitching Pete up."

"But Pete only had six weeks to serve before he was due to be released," I reminded Mick, "and he was always as good as gold."

"True, but another screw, a mate of Davis's, reported Pete for stealing a pair of jeans from the stores just a few days before he was due for release. Pete was carted off to segregation and the governor had him transported back to Lincoln nick even before they'd served up tea that night, with another three months added to his sentence."

"So he ended up having to serve another three months?"

"That was six years ago," said Mick. "And Pete's still banged up in Lincoln."

"So how do they manage that?"

"The screws just come up with a new charge every few weeks, so that whenever Pete comes up on report the governor adds another three months to his sentence. My bet is Pete's stuck in Lincoln for the rest of his life. What a liberty."

"But how do they get away with it?" I asked.

"Haven't you been listening to anything I've been saying, Jeff? If two screws say that's what happened, then that's what happened," repeated Mick, "and no con will be able to tell you any different. Understood?"

"Understood," I replied.

On 12 September 2002 Prison Service Instruction No. 47/2002 stated that the

judgment of the European Court of Human Rights in the case of Ezeh & Connors ruled that, where an offense was so extreme as to result in a punishment of additional days, the protections inherent in Article 6 of the European Convention of Human Rights applied. A hearing must be conducted by an independent and impartial tribunal, and prisoners are entitled to legal assistance at such hearings.

Pete Bailey was released from Lincoln prison on 19 October 2002.

A Greek Tragedy

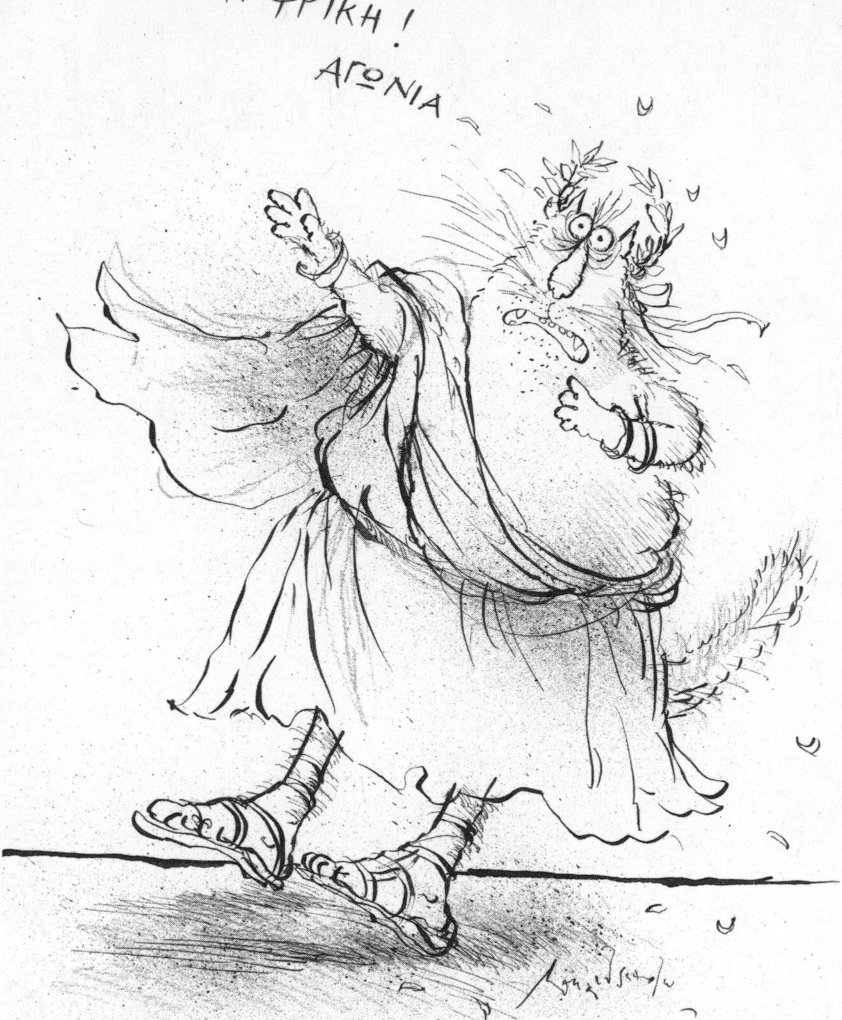
ΤΙ ΦΡΙΚΗ !
ΑΓΩΝΙΑ

George Tsakiris is not one of those Greeks you need to beware of when he is bearing gifts.

George is fortunate enough to spend half his life in London and the other half in his native Athens. He and his two younger brothers, Nicholas and Andrew, run between them a highly successful salvage company, which they inherited from their father.

George and I first met many years ago during a charity function in aid of the Red Cross. His wife Christina was a member of the organizing committee, and she had invited me to be the auctioneer.

At almost every charity auction I have conducted over the years, there has been one item for which you just can't find a buyer, and that night was no exception. On this occasion, another member of the committee had donated a landscape painting that had been daubed by their daughter and would have been orphaned at a village fete. I felt, long before I climbed up onto the rostrum and searched around the room for an opening bid, that I was going to be left stranded once again.

However, I had not taken George's generosity into consideration.

"Do I have an opening bid of one thousand pounds?" I inquired hopefully, but no one came to my rescue. "One thousand?" I repeated, trying not to sound desperate, and just as I was about to give up, out of a sea of black dinner jackets a hand was raised. It was George's.

"Two thousand," I suggested, but no one was interested in my suggestion. "Three thousand," I said looking directly at George. Once again his hand shot up. "Four thousand," I declared confidently, but my confidence was short-lived, so I returned my attention to George. "Five thousand," I demanded, and once again he obliged. Despite his wife being on the committee, I felt enough was enough. "Sold for five thousand pounds, to Mr. George Tsakiris," I announced to loud applause, and a look of relief on Christina's face.

Since then poor George, or to be more accurate rich George, has regularly come to my rescue at such functions, often purchasing ridiculous items, for which I had no hope of arousing even an opening bid. Heaven knows how much I've prised out of the man over the years, all in the name of charity.

Last year, after I'd sold him a trip to Uzbekistan, plus two economy tickets courtesy of Aeroflot, I made my way across to his table to thank him for his generosity.

"No need to thank me," George said as I sat down beside him. "Not a day goes by without me realizing how fortunate I've been, even how lucky I am to be alive."

"Lucky to be alive?" I said, smelling a story.

Let me say at this point that the tired old cliché, that there's a book in every one of us, is a fallacy. However, I have come to accept over the years that most people have experienced a single incident in their life that is unique to them, and well worthy of a short story. George was no exception.

"Lucky to be alive," I repeated.

George and his two brothers divide their business responsibilities equally: George runs the London office, while Nicholas remains in Athens, which allows Andrew to roam around the globe whenever one of their sinking clients needs to be kept afloat.

Although George maintains establishments in London, New York and Saint-Paul-de-Vence, he still regularly returns to the home of the gods, so that he can keep in touch with his large family. Have you noticed how wealthy people always seem to have large families?

At a recent Red Cross Ball, held at the Dorchester, no one came to my rescue when I offered a British Lions' rugby shirt—following their tour of New Zealand—that had been signed by the entire losing team. George was nowhere to be seen, as he'd returned to his native land to attend the wedding of a favorite niece. If it hadn't been for an incident that took place at that wedding, I would never have seen George again. Incidentally, I failed to get even an opening bid for the British Lions' shirt.

George's niece, Isabella, was a native of Cephalonia, one of the most beautiful of the Greek islands, set like a magnificent jewel in the Ionian Sea. Isabella had fallen in love with the son of a local wine grower, and as her father was no longer alive, George had offered to host the wedding reception, which was to be held at the bridegroom's home.

In England it is the custom to invite family and friends to attend the wedding service, followed by a reception, which is often held in a marquee on the lawn of the home of the daughter's parents. When the lawn is not large enough, the festivities are moved to the village hall. After the formal speeches have been delivered, and a reasonable period of time has elapsed, the bride and groom depart for their honeymoon, and fairly soon afterward the guests make their way home.

Leaving a party before midnight is not a tradition the Greeks have come to terms with. They assume that any festivities after a wedding will continue long into the early hours of the following morning, especially when the bridegroom owns a vineyard. Whenever two natives are married on a Greek island, an invitation is automatically extended to the locals so that they can share in a glass of wine and toast the bride's health. Wedding crasher is not an expression that the Greeks are familiar with. The bride's mother doesn't bother sending out gold-embossed cards with RSVP in the lower left-hand corner for one simple reason: no one would bother to reply, but everyone would still turn up.

Another difference between our two great nations is that it is quite unnecessary to hire a marquee or rent the village hall for the festivities, as the Greeks are unlikely to encounter the occasional downpour, especially in the middle of summer—about ten months. Anyone can be a weather forecaster in Greece.

The night before the wedding was due to take place, Christina suggested to her husband that, as host, it might be wise for him to remain sober. Someone, she added, should keep an eye on the proceedings, bearing in mind the bridegroom's occupation. George reluctantly agreed.

The marriage service was held in the island's small church, and the pews were packed with invited, and uninvited, guests long before vespers were chanted. George accepted with his usual grace that he was about to host a rather large gathering. He looked on with pride as his favorite niece and her lover were joined together in holy matrimony. Although Isabella was hidden behind a veil of white lace, her beauty had long been acknowledged by the young men of the island. Her fiancé, Alexis Kulukundis, was tall and slim, and his waistline did not yet bear testament to the fact that he was heir to a vineyard.

And so to the service. Here, for a moment, the English and the Greeks come together, but not for long. The ceremony was conducted by bearded priests attired in long golden surplices and tall black hats. The sweet smell of incense from swinging burners wafted throughout the church, as the priest in the most ornately embroidered gown, who also boasted the longest beard, presided over the marriage, to the accompaniment of murmured psalms and prayers.

George and Christina were among the first to leave the church once the service was over, as they wanted to be back at the house in good time to welcome their guests.

The bridegroom's rambling old farmhouse nestled on the slopes of a hill above the plains of the vineyard. The spacious garden, surrounded by terraced olive groves, was full of chattering well-wishers long before the bride and bridegroom made their entrance.

George must have shaken over two hundred hands, before the appearance of Mr. and Mrs. Kulukundis was announced by a large group of the bridegroom's rowdy friends who were firing pistols into the air in celebration; a Greek tradition which I suspect would not go down well on an English country lawn, and certainly not in the village hall.

With the exception of the immediate family and those guests selected to sit on the long top table by the side of the dance floor, there were, in fact, very few people George had ever set eyes on before.

George took his place at the center of the top table, with Isabella on his right and Alexis on his left. Once they were all seated, course after course of overladen dishes was set before his guests, and the wine flowed as if it were a Bacchanalian orgy rather than a small island wedding. But then Bacchus—the god of wine—was a Greek.

When, in the distance, the cathedral clock chimed eleven times, George hinted to the best man that perhaps the time had come for him to make his speech. Unlike George, he *was* drunk, and certainly wouldn't be able to recall his words the following morning.

The groom followed, and when he tried to express how fortunate he was to have married such a wonderful girl, once again his young friends leaped onto the dance floor and fired their pistols in the air.

George was the final speaker. Aware of the late hour, the pleading look in his guests' eyes, and the half-empty bottles littering the tables around him, he satisfied himself with wishing the bride and groom a blessed life, a euphemism for lots of children. He then invited those who still could to rise and toast the health of the bride and groom. Isabella and Alexis, they all cried, if not in unison.

Once the applause had died down, the band struck up. The groom immediately rose from his place, and, turning to his bride, asked her for the first dance. The newly married couple stepped onto the dance floor, accompanied by another volley of gunfire. The groom's parents followed next, and a few minutes later George and Christina joined them.

Once George had danced with his wife, the bride and the groom's mother, he made his way back to his place in the center seat of the top table, shaking hands along the way with the many guests who wished to thank him.

George was pouring himself a glass of red wine—after all, he had performed all his official duties—when the old man appeared.

George leaped to his feet the moment he saw him standing alone at the entrance to the garden. He placed his glass back on the table and walked quickly across the lawn to welcome the unexpected guest.

Andreas Nikolaides leaned heavily on his two walking sticks. George didn't like to think how long it must have taken the old man to climb up the path from his little cottage, halfway down the mountain. George bowed low and greeted a man who was a legend on the island of Cephalonia as well as in the streets of Athens, despite the fact that he had never once left his native soil. Whenever Andreas was asked why, he simply replied, "Why would anyone leave Paradise?"

In 1942, when the island of Cephalonia had been overrun by the Germans, Andreas Nikolaides escaped to the hills and, at the age of twenty-three, became the leader of the resistance movement. He never left those hills during the long occupation of his homeland and, despite a handsome bounty being placed on his head, did not return to his people until, like Alexander, he had driven the intruders back into the sea.

Once peace was declared in 1945, Andreas returned in triumph. He was elected mayor of Cephalonia, a position which he held, unopposed, for the next thirty years. Now that he was well into his eighties, there wasn't a family on Cephalonia who did not feel in debt to him, and few who didn't claim to be a relative.

"Good evening, sir," said George stepping forward to greet the old man. "We are honored by your presence at my niece's wedding."

"It is I who should be honored," replied Andreas, returning the bow. "Your niece's grandfather fought and died by my side. In any case," he added with a wink, "it's an old man's prerogative to kiss every new bride on the island."

George guided his distinguished guest slowly round the outside of the dance floor and on toward the top table. Guests stopped dancing and applauded as the old man passed by. George insisted that Andreas take his place in the center of the top table, so that he could be seated between the bride and groom. Andreas reluctantly took his host's place of honor. When Isabella turned to see who had been placed next to her, she burst into tears and threw her arms around the old man. "Your presence has made the wedding complete," she said.

Andreas smiled and, looking up at George, whispered, "I only wish I'd had that effect on women when I was younger."

George left Andreas seated in his place at the center of the top table, chatting happily to the bride and groom. He picked up a plate and walked slowly down a table laden with food. George took his time selecting only the most delicate morsels that he felt the old man would find easy to digest. Finally he chose a bottle of vintage wine from a case that his own father had presented to him on the day of his wedding. George turned back to take the offering to his honored guest just as the chimes on the cathedral clock struck twelve, hailing the dawn of a new day.

Once more, the young men of the island charged onto the dance floor and fired their pistols into the air, to the cheers of the assembled guests. George frowned, but then for a moment recalled his own youth. Carrying the plate in one hand and a bottle of wine in the other, he continued walking back toward his place in the center of the table, now occupied by Andreas Nikolaides.

Suddenly, without warning, one of the young bandoliers, who'd had a little too much to drink, ran forward and tripped on the edge of the dance floor, just as he was discharging his last shot. George froze in horror when he saw the old man slump forward in his chair, his head falling onto the table. George dropped the bottle of wine and the plate of food onto the grass as the bride screamed. He ran quickly to the center of the table, but it was too late. Andreas Nikolaides was already dead.

The large, exuberant gathering was suddenly in turmoil, some screaming, some weeping, while others fell to their knees, but the majority were hushed into a shocked, somber silence, unable to grasp what had taken place.

George bent down over the body and lifted the old man into his arms. He carried him slowly across the lawn, the guests forming a corridor of bowed heads, as he walked toward the house.

George had just bid five thousand pounds for two seats at a West End musical that had already closed when he told me the story of Andreas Nikolaides.

"They say of Andreas that he saved the life of everyone on that island," George remarked as he raised his glass in memory of the old man. He paused before adding, "Mine included."

The Commissioner

"Why does he want to see me?" asked the Commissioner.

"He says it's a personal matter."

"How long has he been out of prison?"

The Commissioner's secretary glanced down at Raj Malik's file. "He was released six weeks ago."

Naresh Kumar stood up, pushed back his chair and began pacing around the room; something he always did whenever he needed to think a problem through. He had convinced himself—well, almost—that by regularly walking round the office he was carrying out some form of exercise. Long gone were the days when he could play a game of hockey in the afternoon, three games of squash the same evening and then jog back to police headquarters. With each new promotion, more silver braid had been sewn on his epaulet and more inches appeared around his waist.

"Once I've retired and have more time, I'll start training again," he told his number two, Anil Khan. Neither of them believed it.

The Commissioner stopped to stare out of the window and look down on the teeming streets of Mumbai some fourteen floors below him: ten million inhabitants who ranged from some of the poorest to some of the wealthiest people on earth. From beggars to billionaires, and it was his responsibility to police all of them. His predecessor had left him with the words: "At best, you can hope to keep the lid on the kettle." In less than a year, when he passed on the responsibility to his deputy, he would be proffering the same advice.

Naresh Kumar had been a policeman all his life, like his father before him, and what he most enjoyed about the job was its sheer unpredictability. Today was no different, although a great deal had changed since the time when you could clip a child across the ear if you caught him stealing a mango. If you tried that today, the parents would sue you for assault and the child would claim he needed counseling. But, fortunately, his deputy Anil Khan had come to accept that guns on the street, drug dealers and the war against terrorism were all part of a modern policeman's lot.

The Commissioner's thoughts returned to Raj Malik, a man he'd been responsible for sending to prison on three occasions in the past thirty years. Why did the old con want to see him? There was only one way he was going to find out. He turned to face his secretary. "Make an appointment for me to see Malik, but only allocate him fifteen minutes."

The Commissioner had forgotten that he'd agreed to see Malik until his secretary placed the file on his desk a few minutes before he was due to arrive.

"If he's one minute late," said the Commissioner, "cancel the appointment."

"He's already waiting in the lobby, sir," she replied.

Kumar frowned, and flicked open the file. He began to familiarize himself with Malik's criminal record, most of which he was able to recall because on two occasions—one when he had been a detective sergeant, and the second, a newly promoted inspector— he had been the arresting officer.

Malik was a white-collar criminal who was well capable of holding down a serious job. However, as a young man he had quickly discovered that he possessed enough charm and native cunning to con naive people, particularly old ladies, out of large sums of money, without having to exert a great deal of effort.

His first scam was not unique to Mumbai. All he required was a small printing press, some headed notepaper and a list of widows. Once he'd obtained the latter—on a daily basis from the obituary column of the *Mumbai Times*—he was in business. He specialized in selling shares in overseas companies that didn't exist. This provided him with a regular income, until he tried to sell some stock to the widow of another conman.

When Malik was charged, he admitted to having made over a million rupees, but the Commissioner suspected that it was a far larger sum; after all, how many widows were willing to admit they had been taken in by Malik's charms? Malik was sentenced to five years in Pune jail and Kumar lost touch with him for nearly a decade.

Malik was back inside again after he'd been arrested for selling flats in a high-rise apartment block on land that turned out to be a swamp. This time the judge sent him down for seven years. Another decade passed.

Malik's third offense was even more ingenious, and resulted in an even longer sentence. He appointed himself a life-assurance broker. Unfortunately the annuities never matured—except for Malik.

His barrister suggested to the presiding judge that his client had cleared around twelve million rupees, but as little of the money was available to be given back to those who were still living, the judge felt that twelve years would be a fair return on this particular policy.

By the time the Commissioner had turned the last page, he was still puzzled as to why Malik could possibly want to see him. He pressed a button under the desk to alert his secretary that he was ready for his next appointment.

Commissioner Kumar glanced up as the door opened. He stared at a man he barely recognized. Malik must have been ten years younger than he was, but they would have passed for contemporaries. Although Malik's file stated that he was five foot nine and weighed a hundred and seventy pounds, the man who walked into his office did not fit that description.

The old con's skin was lined and parched, and his back was hunched, making him appear small and shrunken. Half a life spent in jail had taken its toll. He wore a white shirt that was frayed at the collar and cuffs, and a baggy suit that might at some

time in the past have been tailored for him. This was not the self-confident man the Commissioner had first arrested over thirty years ago, a man who always had an answer for everything.

Malik gave the Commissioner a weak smile as he came to a halt in front of him.

"Thank you for agreeing to see me, sir," he said quietly. Even his voice had shrunk.

The Commissioner nodded, waved him to the chair on the other side of his desk and said, "I have a busy morning ahead of me, Malik, so perhaps you could get straight to the point."

"Of course, sir," Malik replied, even before he'd sat down. "It's simply that I am looking for a job."

The Commissioner had considered many reasons why Malik might want to see him, but seeking employment had not been among them.

"Before you laugh," continued Malik, "please allow me to put my case."

The Commissioner leaned back in his chair and placed the tips of his fingers together, as if in silent prayer.

"I have spent too much of my life in jail," said Malik. He paused. "I've recently reached the age of fifty, and can assure you that I have no desire to go back inside again."

The Commissioner nodded, but didn't express an opinion.

"Last week, Commissioner," continued Malik, "you addressed the annual general meeting of the Mumbai Chamber of Commerce. I read your speech in the *Times* with great interest. You expressed the view to the leading businessmen of this city that they should consider employing people who had served a prison sentence—give them a second chance, you said, or they will simply take the easy option and return to a life of crime. A sentiment I was able to agree with."

"But I also pointed out," interrupted the Commissioner, "that I was only referring to first offenders."

"Exactly my point," countered Malik. "If you consider there is a problem for first offenders, just imagine what I come up against, when I apply for a job." Malik paused and straightened his tie before he continued. "If your speech was sincere and not just delivered for public consumption, then perhaps you should heed your own advice, and lead by example."

"And what did you have in mind?" asked the Commissioner. "Because you certainly do not possess the ideal qualifications for police work."

Malik ignored the Commissioner's sarcasm and plowed boldly on. "In the same paper in which your speech was reported, there was an advertisement for a filing clerk in your records department. I began life as a clerk for the P & O Shipping Company, right here in this city. I think that you will find, were you to check the records, that I carried out that job with enthusiasm and efficiency, and on that occasion left with an unblemished record."

"But that was over thirty years ago," said the Commissioner, not needing to refer to the file in front of him.

"Then I will have to end my career as I began it," replied Malik, "as a filing clerk."

The Commissioner didn't speak for some time while he considered Malik's proposition. He finally leaned forward, placed his hands on the desk, and said, "I will give some thought to your request, Malik. Does my secretary know how to get in touch with you?"

"Yes, she does, sir," Malik replied as he rose from his place. "Every night I can be found at the YMCA hostel on Victoria Street." He paused. "I have no plans to move in the near future."

Over lunch in the officers' dining room, Commissioner Kumar briefed his deputy on the meeting with Malik.

Anil Khan burst out laughing. "Hoist with your own petard, Chief," he said with considerable feeling.

"True enough," replied the Commissioner as he helped himself to another spoonful of rice, "and when you take over from me next year, this little episode will serve to remind you of the consequences of your words, especially when they are delivered in public."

"Does that mean that you are seriously considering employing the man?" asked Khan, as he stared across the table at his boss.

"Possibly," replied Kumar. "Why, are you against the idea?"

"You are in your last year as Commissioner," Khan reminded him, "with an enviable reputation for probity and competence. Why take a risk that might jeopardize such a fine record?"

"I feel that's a little over-dramatic," said the Commissioner. "Malik's a broken man, which you would have seen for yourself had you been present at the meeting."

"Once a conman, always a conman," replied Khan. "So I repeat, why take the risk?"

"Perhaps because it's the correct course of action, given the circumstances," replied the Commissioner. "If I turn Malik down, why should anyone bother to listen to my opinion ever again?"

"But a filing clerk's job is particularly sensitive," remonstrated Khan. "Malik would have access to information that should only be seen by those whose discretion is not in question."

"I've already considered that," said the Commissioner. "We have two filing departments: one in this building, which is, as you rightly point out, highly sensitive, and another based on the outskirts of the city that deals only with dead cases, which have either been solved or are no longer being followed up."

"I still wouldn't risk it," said Khan as he placed his knife and fork back on the plate.

"I've cut down the risk even more," responded the Commissioner. "I'm going to place Malik on a month's trial. A supervisor will keep a close eye on him, and then report directly back to me. Should Malik put so much as a toe over the line, he'll be back on the street the same day."

"I still wouldn't risk it," repeated Khan.

On the first of the month, Raj Malik reported for work at the police records department on 47 Mahatma Drive, on the outskirts of the city. His hours were eight a.m. to six p.m. six days a week, with a salary of nine hundred rupees a month. Malik's daily responsibility was to visit every police station in the outer district, on his bicycle, and collect any dead files. He would then pass them over to his supervisor, who would file them away in the basement, rarely to be referred to again.

At the end of his first month, Malik's supervisor reported back to the Commissioner as instructed. "I wish I had a dozen Maliks," he told the chief. "Unlike today's young, he's always on time, doesn't take extended breaks, and never complains when you ask him to do something not covered by his job description. With your permission," the supervisor added, "I would like to put his pay up to one thousand rupees a month."

The supervisor's second report was even more glowing. "I lost a member of staff through illness last week, and Malik took over several of his responsibilities and somehow still managed to cover both jobs."

The supervisor's report at the end of Malik's third month was so flattering that when the Commissioner addressed the annual dinner of the Mumbai Rotary Club, not only did he appeal to its members to reach out their hands to ex-offenders, but he went on to assure his audience that he had heeded his own advice and been able to prove one of his long-held theories. *If you give former prisoners a real chance, they won't reoffend.*

The following day, the *Mumbai Times* ran the headline:

COMMISSIONER LEADS BY EXAMPLE

Kumar's sentiments were reported in great detail, alongside a photo of Raj Malik, with the byline, *a reformed character*. The Commissioner placed the article on his deputy's desk.

Malik waited until his supervisor had left for his lunch break. He always drove home just after twelve and spent an hour with his wife. Malik watched as his boss's car disappeared out of sight before he slipped back down to the basement. He placed a stack of papers that needed to be filed on the corner of the counter, just in case someone came in unannounced and asked what he was up to.

He then walked across to the old wooden

cabinets that were stacked one on top of the other. He bent down and pulled open one of the files. After nine months he had reached the letter P and still hadn't come across the ideal candidate. He had already thumbed through dozens of Patels during the previous week, dismissing most of them as either irrelevant or inconsequential for what he had in mind. That was until he reached one with the first initials H.H.

Malik removed the thick file from the cabinet, placed it on the counter top and slowly began to turn the pages. He didn't need to read the details a second time to know that he'd hit the jackpot.

He scribbled down the name, address and telephone numbers neatly on a slip of paper, and then returned the file to its place in the cabinet. He smiled. During his tea break, Malik would call and make an appointment to see Mr. H.H. Patel.

With only a few weeks to go before his retirement, Commissioner Kumar had quite forgotten about his prodigy. That was until he received a call from Mr. H.H. Patel, one of the city's leading bankers. Mr. Patel was requesting an urgent meeting with the Commissioner—to discuss a personal matter.

Commissioner Kumar looked upon H.H. not only as a friend, but as a man of integrity, and certainly not someone who would use the word urgent without good reason.

Kumar rose from behind his desk as Mr. Patel entered the room. He ushered his old friend to a comfortable chair in the corner of the room and pressed a button under his desk. Moments later his secretary appeared with a pot of tea and a plate of Bath Oliver biscuits. The Deputy Commissioner followed in her wake.

"I thought it might be wise to have Anil Khan present for this meeting, H.H., as he will be taking over from me in a few weeks' time."

"I know of your reputation, of course," said Mr. Patel, shaking Khan warmly by the hand, "and I am delighted that you are able to join us."

Once the secretary had served the three men with tea, she left the room. The moment the door was closed, Commissioner Kumar dispensed with any more small talk.

"You asked to see me urgently, H.H., concerning a personal matter.'

"Yes," replied Patel. "I thought you ought to know that I had a visit yesterday from someone who claims to work for you."

The Commissioner raised an eyebrow.

"A Mr. Raj Malik."

"He is a junior filing clerk in the—"

"In a private capacity, he was at pains to emphasize."

The Commissioner began tapping the armrest of his chair with the palm of his right hand, as Patel continued. "Malik said that you were in possession of a file that showed that I was under investigation for money laundering."

"You were, H.H.," said the Commissioner, with his usual candor. "Following nine/eleven, the Minister of Internal Affairs instructed me to investigate any organization which dealt in large sums of cash. That included casinos, racetracks and, in your case, the Bank of Mumbai. A member of my team interviewed your chief teller and advised him about what he should be on the lookout for, and I personally signed the clearance certificate for your company."

"I remember, you briefed me at the time," said Patel, "but your fellow, Malik—"

"He's not my fellow."

"—said that he could arrange to have my file destroyed." He paused. "For a small consideration."

"He said what?" said Kumar almost exploding out of his chair.

"How small?" asked Deputy Commissioner Khan calmly.

"Ten million rupees," replied Patel.

"H.H., I don't know what to say," said the Commissioner.

"You don't have to say anything," said Patel, "because it never crossed my mind, even for a moment, that you could be involved in anything quite so stupid, and I told Malik as much."

"I am grateful," said the Commissioner.

"No need to be," said Patel, "but I did think that perhaps others, less charitable . . ." He paused. "Especially as Malik's visit came so close to your retirement . . ." He hesitated again. "And were the press to get hold of the story, it might so easily be misunderstood."

"I am grateful for your concern, and the speed with which you have acted," said Kumar. "I will remain eternally in your debt."

"I want nothing more than to be sure that this city rightly remains eternally in your debt," said Patel, "so that when you leave office it will be in a blaze of glory, rather than with question marks hanging over your head, which, as we both know, would linger on long after your retirement."

The Deputy Commissioner nodded his agreement as Patel rose from his place.

"You know, Naresh," Patel said, turning to face the Commissioner, "I would never have agreed to see the damn man, if you had not spoken so highly of him in your speech to the Rotary Club last month. He even produced the article in the *Mumbai Times*. I therefore assumed that the fellow had come with your blessing." Mr. Patel turned to face Khan. "May I wish you luck when you take over as Commissioner," he added, shaking hands with the deputy. "I don't envy you having to follow such a fine man." Kumar smiled for the first time that morning.

"I'll be back in a moment," the Commissioner said to his deputy as he left his office to accompany Patel to the front door.

The Deputy Commissioner stared out of the window as he waited for the Chief to return. He munched on a biscuit as he mulled over several possible alternatives. By the time the Commissioner walked back into the room, Khan knew exactly what had to be done. But would he be able to convince his boss this time?

"I'll have Malik arrested and behind bars within the hour," said the Commissioner as he picked up the phone on his desk.

"I wonder, sir," said Deputy Khan quietly, "if that's the best course of action—given the circumstances?"

"I don't have much choice," said the Commissioner as he began dialing.

"You may be right," said Khan, "but before you make such an irrevocable decision, perhaps we should consider how this is all going to play—" he paused—"with the press."

"They'll have a field day," said Kumar as he replaced the phone and began pacing around the room. "They won't be able to make up their minds if I should be hanged as a crook who's willing to accept bribes, or dismissed as the most naive fool ever to hold the office of Commissioner. Neither scenario bears thinking about."

"But we have to think about it," insisted

Deputy Khan, "because your enemies—and even good men have enemies—will happily settle for someone who's willing to take kickbacks, while your friends will not be able to deny the lesser charge of naivety."

"But surely after forty years of service, people will believe . . ."

"People will believe whatever they want to believe," said Khan, confirming the Commissioner's worst fears, "and certainly you won't be able to send Malik back to prison until he's been given the chance to appear in a witness box and tell the world his side of the story."

"But who would believe that old—"

"No smoke without fire, they'll be whispering in the corridors of the law courts, and that will be tame compared with the headlines in the morning papers once Malik has spent a couple of days in the witness box being questioned by a friendly barrister who sees you as nothing more than a stepping stone in his career."

Kumar continued to pace around the room, but didn't respond.

"Let me try and second-guess the headlines that would follow such a cross-examination." Khan paused before saying,

" 'Commissioner accepts bribes to destroy friends' files' might be the headline in the *Times*, while the tabloids will surely be a little more colorful—'Bung money left in Commissioner's office by delivery boy,' or perhaps 'Commissioner Kumar employs ex-con to carry out his dirty work?' "

"I think I've got the picture," said the Commissioner, as he sank back into the chair next to Khan. "So what the hell am I supposed to do about it?"

"What you've always done in the past," Khan replied. "Play it by the book."

The Commissioner looked across at his deputy quizzically. "What do you have in mind?"

"Malik," shouted the supervisor at the top of his voice, even before he'd put the phone down. " Commissioner Kumar wants to see you, immediately."

"Did he say why?" asked Malik nervously.

"No, he's not in the habit of confiding in me," replied the supervisor, "but don't hang about because he's not a man who likes to be kept waiting."

"Yes, sir," Malik replied. He closed the file

he'd been working on and placed it back on the supervisor's desk. He walked across to his locker, removed his bicycle clips and left the building without another word. It wasn't until he was outside on the pavement that he began to shake. Had they caught on to his latest scam? Not that it had proved that successful. He unlocked the chain that was attached to the railings and began to consider his options. Should he make a run for it, or simply try to brazen it out? He hadn't been left with a lot of choice. After all, where would he run to? And even if he did decide to run, it would only be a matter of days, perhaps hours, before they caught up with him.

Malik slipped on his bicycle clips, mounted his third-hand Raleigh Lenton and began to pedal slowly toward the city center. The dusty brown roads were teeming with other bicycles, cars and countless numbers of people, all heading in different directions. The incessant honking of horns, the multitude of different smells, the beating down of the sun and the bustle of everyday life ensured that Mumbai was like no other city on earth. Street traders thrust out their arms as Malik passed, trying to sell him their wares, while beggars with no arms ran by his side, not assisting his progress. Should he come clean and admit what he'd been up to?

He cycled for a few more yards. No, never admit to anything, a golden rule that he'd learned after long years in prison. He swerved to avoid a cow and nearly fell off.

Assume they know nothing until you're cornered. Even then, deny everything. As he rounded the next corner, police headquarters loomed up in front of him. If he was going to make a dash for it, it would have to be now or never. He pedalled on, until he was only a few yards away from the steps leading up to the front entrance. He tugged firmly on the tired brake handles until his bike came to a slow, unsteady halt. He climbed off, and padlocked his one asset to the nearest railing. He walked slowly up the steps to police headquarters, pushed his way through the swing doors and headed nervously toward the reception desk. He told the duty officer his name. Perhaps there had been a mistake.

"I have an appointment with—"

"Ah, yes," the duty officer replied ominously, without needing to consult his roster. "The Commissioner is waiting to see you. You'll find his office is on the fourteenth floor."

Malik turned and began walking toward the lifts, aware that the duty officer's eyes never left him. Malik glanced at the front door. This would be his last chance to escape, he thought, as the doors of one of the lifts slid open. He stepped into a crowded elevator, which made several stops on its slow interrupted journey to the fourteenth floor. By the time Malik reached the top floor, he was sweating profusely, and it wasn't just the crowded space and lack of air conditioning that caused his unease.

When the doors finally parted, he was on his own. Malik stepped out onto the only thickly carpeted corridor in the building. He looked around and then recalled his last visit. He began to walk slowly toward an office at the far end of the corridor. The word Commissioner was printed in bold stencilled letters on the door.

Malik knocked quietly—perhaps something more important had arisen, causing the Commissioner to leave the office without warning. He heard a female voice invite him to enter. He opened the door to find the Commissioner's secretary seated behind her desk, tapping away furiously. She stopped typing the moment she saw Malik.

"The Commissioner is expecting you," was all she offered. She didn't smile and she didn't frown as she rose from her place. Perhaps she was unaware of his fate. The secretary disappeared through another door and returned almost immediately. "The Commissioner will see you now, Mr. Malik," she said, and held the door open for him.

Malik walked into the Commissioner's office, to find him seated at his desk, eyes down, studying an open file. He raised his head, looked directly at him and said, "Have a seat, Malik." Not Raj, not Mr., just Malik.

Malik slipped into the chair opposite the Commissioner. He sat in silence, trying not to appear nervous as he watched the second hand of the clock on the wall behind the desk complete a full minute.

"Malik," the Commissioner eventually said as he looked up from the papers on his desk, "I've just been reading your supervisor's annual report."

Malik remained silent, although he could feel a bead of sweat trickling down his nose.

The Commissioner looked back down again. "He's very complimentary about your work," said Kumar, "full of praise. Far better than I could have hoped for when you sat in that chair just a year ago." The Commissioner looked up and smiled. "In fact, he's recommending that you should be promoted."

"Promoted?" said Malik in disbelief.

"Yes, though it may not prove that easy, as there are not too many appropriate jobs available at the present time. However, I do believe I have come across a position that is ideally suited for your particular talents."

"Oh, thank you, sir," said Malik, relaxing for the first time.

"There is a vacancy—" the Commissioner opened another file and smiled—"for an assistant in the city morgue." He extracted a single sheet of paper and began reading from it.

"It would be your responsibility to scrub the blood off the slabs and clean the floor immediately after the bodies have been dissected and stored away. I'm told the stench is not all that pleasant, but a face mask is supplied, and I have no doubt that, in time, one gets used to it." He continued to smile at Malik. "The appointment comes with the rank of sub-supervisor, along with a corresponding rise in salary. It also has other perks, not least that you would have your own room directly above the morgue, so you wouldn't have to bed down any longer at the YMCA." The Commissioner paused. "And, should you continue to hold the post until your sixtieth birthday, you would also be entitled to a modest pension." The Commissioner closed Malik's file and looked directly at him. "Any questions?" he asked.

"Only one, sir," said Malik. "Is there any alternative?"

"Oh, yes," replied the Commissioner. "You can spend the rest of your life in jail."

In the Eye of the Beholder

Other than the fact that they had been to school together, the two of them had little in common.

Gian Lorenzo Venici had been a diligent child since his first roll call at the age of five, whereas Paolo Castelli somehow managed always to be late, even for his first roll call.

Gian Lorenzo felt at home in the classroom with books, essays and exams, where he outshone his contemporaries. Paolo achieved the same results on the football field, with a change of pace, a deceptive turn and a shot at goal which beguiled his own team as well as the opposition. Both young men progressed to St. Cecilia's, the most prestigious high school in Rome, where they were able to display their talents to a wider audience.

When their school days were over, they both graduated to Roma: Gian Lorenzo to the nation's oldest university as a scholar, Paolo to the nation's oldest football club as a striker. Although they didn't mix in the same circles, they were both well aware of the other's achievements. While Gian Lorenzo collected honors in one field, Paolo won them on another, both achieving their goals.

After leaving university, Gian Lorenzo joined his father at the Venici Gallery. He immediately set about converting those years of study into something more practical, as he wished to emulate his father and become the most respected art dealer in Italy.

By the time Gian Lorenzo had begun his apprenticeship, Paolo had been appointed captain of Roma. With the cheers and adulation of the fans ringing in his ears, he led them to championship and European glory. Gian Lorenzo only had to turn to the back pages of any newspaper, on an almost daily basis, to follow the exploits of his former classmate, and to the gossip columns to discover who was the latest beauty to be found dangling from his arm: another difference between them.

Gian Lorenzo quickly discovered that in his chosen profession long-term reputation would be built not on the occasional inspired goal, but on hours of dedicated research, combined with good judgment. He had inherited from his father the two most important gifts in any art dealer's armory—a good eye and a good nose. Antonio Venici also taught his son not only how to look, but *where* to look, when searching for a masterpiece. The old man only dealt in the finest examples of Renaissance painting and sculpture, which would never appear on the open market. Unless a piece was exclusive, Antonio didn't venture out of his gallery. His son followed in his footsteps. The gallery bought and sold only three, perhaps four, paintings a year, but those masters changed hands at around the same price as one of Roma's strikers. After forty years in the business, Gian Lorenzo's father knew not only who possessed the great collections, but more important, who might be willing or, better still, needed to part with the occasional masterpiece.

Gian Lorenzo became so engrossed in his work that he missed the injury Paolo Castelli sustained while playing for Italy against Spain in the European Cup. This personal setback placed Paolo on the side-lines of the football field, as well as the newspapers, especially when it became clear that he had reached his sell-by date.

Paolo left the world stage just as Gian Lorenzo strode onto it. He began to travel around Europe representing the gallery in an endless quest to seek out only the rarest ex-amples of genius, and, having acquired a masterpiece, to find someone who could af-ford to purchase it.

Gian Lorenzo often wondered what had become of Paolo since he'd stopped play-ing football and the press no longer re-ported his every move. He was to discover overnight when Paolo announced his en-gagement.

Paolo's choice of marriage partner en-sured that his exploits were transferred from the back pages to the front.

Angelina Porcelli was the only daughter

of Massimo Porcelli, president of Roma Football Club and chairman of Ulitox, the largest pharmaceutical company in Italy. *A marriage of two heavyweights*, declared the banner headline in one of the tabloids.

Gian Lorenzo turned to page three to discover what merited such a comment. Paolo's bride-to-be was six foot two—an advantage for a model, I hear you say—but there the comparison ended, because the other vital statistic the reporters latched on to was Angelina's weight. This seemed to vary between three hundred and three hundred and fifty pounds, according to whether it was reported by a broadsheet or a tabloid.

A picture is worth a thousand words. Gian Lorenzo studied several photographs of Angelina, and concluded that only Rubens would have considered her as a model. In every picture of Paolo's future bride, no amount of skill displayed by the couturiers of Milan, the stylists of Paris, the jewelers of London, not to mention the legions of personal trainers, dietitians and masseurs, was able to transform her image from sugar plum fairy to prima ballerina. Whichever angle the photographers took, however considerate they tried to be, and some didn't, they only emphasized the transparent difference between her and her fiancé, especially when she stood alongside Roma's former hero. The Italian press, clearly obsessed by Angelina's size, reported nothing else about her of any interest.

Gian Lorenzo turned to the arts pages,

and had quite forgotten about Paolo and his
future bride when he strode into the gallery
later that morning. As he opened the door
to his office, he was greeted by his secretary, who thrust a large, gold-embossed
card into his hand. Gian Lorenzo glanced
down at the invitation.

**Signor Massimo Porcelli
has pleasure in inviting**

Gian Lorenzo Venici

**to the marriage of his daughter,
Angelina,
to Signor Paolo Castelli
at the Villa Borghese.**

Six weeks later Gian Lorenzo joined a
thousand guests in the grounds of the Villa
Borghese. It soon became clear that
Signor Porcelli was determined his only
child would enjoy a wedding that not only
she, but everyone else present, would
never forget.

The setting in the Borghese Gardens, perched on one of the seven hills overlooking Rome, with its imposing terracotta and cream villa in the background, was the stuff of fairytales. Gian Lorenzo strolled around the grounds, admiring the sculptures and fountains while catching up with old friends and contemporaries, some of whom he had not seen since his school days. Some twenty minutes before the ceremony was due to take place, a dozen liveried ushers, in long blue coats trimmed with gold braid and wearing white wigs, moved among the throng. They invited the guests to take their seats in the rose garden as the wedding ceremony was about to commence.

Gian Lorenzo joined a large crowd as they made their way toward a recently constructed stand with an elevated semi-circle of seats surrounding a raised stage with an altar as its centerpiece; not unlike a football ground where a different form of worship takes place on a Saturday afternoon. His connoisseur's eye took in the magnificent view over Rome, a scene made even more dazzling by the number of beautiful women, dressed in clothes that he suspected had never been worn before, and in some cases would never be worn again. They were complemented by elegantly dressed men in tailcoats and white shirts, with only different colored ties and cravats to suggest the peacock in them. Gian Lorenzo looked around to find that he was surrounded by leading politicians, captains of industry, actors, socialites, as well as many of Paolo's old teammates.

The next actor to take his place on the stage was Paolo himself, accompanied by his best man. Gian Lorenzo knew he was a well-known footballer, but couldn't recall his name. As Paolo strode down the grass path and onto the pitch, Gian Lorenzo understood only too well why women could not take their eyes off the man. Paolo walked up onto the stage, took his place on the right of the altar and waited to be joined by his bride.

A forty-piece string orchestra, almost hidden among the trees behind the altar, struck up the opening chords of Mendelssohn's Wedding March. A thousand guests rose from their seats and turned to see the bride as she progressed slowly up the thick grass carpet on the arm of her proud father.

"What a beautiful dress," said the lady standing in front of Gian Lorenzo. He nodded his agreement and, staring at the yards of Persian silk that formed a magnificent train behind Angelina, didn't express the one thought that must have been on everyone's mind. Nevertheless, the look on Angelina's face was that of a bride displaying total contentment with her lot. She was walking toward the man she adored, aware that many of the women present would have been only too happy to take her place.

As Angelina climbed the steps up onto the stage, the boards creaked. Her future husband smiled as he took a pace forward to join his bride. They both turned to face Cardinal Montagni, the Archbishop of Naples. One or two guests failed to stifle a smile when the cardinal turned to Paolo and inquired, "Do you take this woman to be your lawful wedded wife, for better for worse, for richer for poorer . . ."

Once bride and groom had been joined together in holy matrimony, Gian Lorenzo made his way to the Long Garden, to join a thousand other guests for dinner. A feast followed that began with champagne and truffle risotto, and ended with chocolate soufflé and a Chateau d'Yquem. Gian Lorenzo could barely move by the time Paolo rose to reply to his best man's speech.

"I am the happiest man on earth," he declared, as he turned to face his beaming bride. "I have found the ideal woman for me, and I am only too aware that I must be the envy of every bachelor present." A sentiment which Gian Lorenzo could not quite agree with, but he quickly banished the ungracious thought from his mind. Paolo continued, "You know, I was the first suitor to win Angelina's heart. No longer will I have to search for the perfect woman because I have found her. Please rise and join me in a toast to Angelina, my little angel." The gathering rose as one and toasted, "Angelina." One or two even managed "his little angel."

After the speeches were over, the dancing began to yet another band—this time one that had been flown in from New Orleans. Gian Lorenzo overheard that Angelina had once mentioned to Papa that she liked jazz.

As the band struck up and the champagne continued to flow, the newlyweds moved among their guests, which gave

Gian Lorenzo a fleeting moment to thank Paolo and his bride for including him in such an unforgettable occasion. "Medici would have swooned," he told her, as he kissed her hand. She gave him a warm, gentle smile, but didn't respond.

"Let's keep in touch," suggested Paolo as the two of them drifted away. "Angelina is fascinated by art, you know, and is thinking of starting her own collection," were the last words Gian Lorenzo heard, before Paolo moved on to another guest.

Just before the sun rose and breakfast was about to be served, Signor and Signora Castelli set off for the airport, with a thousand hands waving their farewells. They drove out of the grounds of the Borghese with Paolo at the wheel of his latest Ferrari—not the ideal car for his bride. When they reached the airport, Paolo drove out onto a private airstrip and brought the car to a halt by the side of a Lear jet that was waiting for two passengers. The newlyweds left the Ferrari parked on the runway, climbed the steps and disappeared inside Papa's aircraft. Within minutes of fastening their seatbelts, the jet took off for Acapulco,

the first stop on their three-month honeymoon.

Despite Paolo's parting words, when the
Castellis returned from their honeymoon
they made no attempt to keep in touch with
Gian Lorenzo. However, he was able to follow their exploits on an almost daily basis in
the gossip columns of the national press.

A year later he read that they would be
moving to Venice, where they had purchased the type of villa that makes the covers, not the inside pages, of glossy
magazines. Gian Lorenzo assumed that he
and his old friend were unlikely to bump into
each other again.

When Antonio Venici retired, he happily
handed over the responsibility for the family
business to his son. As the new owner of
the Venici Gallery, Gian Lorenzo spent half
his time traveling around Europe in search
of that elusive painting which makes collectors gasp, while not insulting the dealer with
any suggestion of bargaining.

One such journey was to Venice, to view
a Canaletto owned by the Contessa di
Palma—a lady who, having divorced her

third husband and sadly no longer possessing the looks to guarantee a fourth, had decided she would have to part with one or two of her treasures. The Contessa's only stipulation was that no one must discover that she was facing temporary financial difficulties. Every leading dealer in Italy knew of her mounting debts and unpaid creditors. Gian Lorenzo was only thankful that the Contessa had chosen him to share her confidences with.

Gian Lorenzo took some time to study the Contessa's considerable collection and concluded that she had an eye not only for rich men. After he had agreed a price for the Canaletto, he expressed the hope that this might be the beginning of a long and fruitful relationship.

"Let's start with dinner at Harry's Bar, my darling," said the Contessa, once she had Gian Lorenzo's check in her hand.

Gian Lorenzo was making up his mind between an affogato or an espresso when Paolo and Angelina strolled into Harry's Bar. Everyone in the room followed their progress, as the maître d' ushered them unctuously to a corner table.

"Now there's someone who can afford to

buy my *entire* collection," whispered the Contessa.

"Without a doubt," agreed Gian Lorenzo, "but unfortunately Paolo only collects rare cars."

"And even rarer women," interjected the Contessa.

"And I'm not altogether sure what Angelina collects."

"A few extra pounds each year," suggested the Contessa. "She once came to tea with my second husband and literally ate us out of house and home. By the time she left we were down to the water biscuits."

"Well, let's try and make up for that tonight," said Gian Lorenzo. "I'm told the zabaglione is their signature dish?"

The Contessa showed no interest in the zabaglione, but simply sailed on, ignoring her companion's unsubtle hint. "Can you imagine what those two get up to, when they're in bed?"

Gian Lorenzo was surprised that the Contessa was willing to voice a question he had often thought about but never felt able to express. And there was worse to come as the Contessa went on to describe things that hadn't, until then, even crossed Gian Lorenzo's mind.

"Do you think he climbs on top of her?" Gian Lorenzo didn't offer an opinion. "A feat in itself," she continued, "because if they did it the other way round, surely she'd suffocate him."

Gian Lorenzo didn't care to think about the image, so he tried once again to change the subject. "We went to the same school, you know—one hell of an athlete."

"You'd have to be, to satisfy her."

"I even attended their wedding," he added. "A truly memorable occasion, though I doubt after all this time that he would even remember I was among the guests."

"Would you really be willing to spend the rest of your life with such a creature, however much money she had to offer?" asked the Contessa, not paying attention to her host's words.

"He claims to adore her," said Gian Lorenzo, "calls her his little angel."

"In that case, I wouldn't want to meet up with his idea of a big angel."

"But if he felt otherwise," suggested Gian Lorenzo, "he could always divorce her."

"Not a chance," said the Contessa, "you clearly haven't been told about their pre-nuptial agreement."

"No, I haven't," admitted Gian Lorenzo, trying not to sound interested.

"Her father had much the same opinion of that clapped-out footballer as I do. Old man Porcelli made him sign an agreement which spelled out that if Paolo ever divorced his daughter he would end up with nothing. Paolo was also forced to sign a second document stating that he would never reveal the contents of the pre-nuptial to anyone, including Angelina."

"Then how do you know about it?" prompted Gian Lorenzo.

"When you've signed as many pre-nuptials as I have, darling, you hear things."

Gian Lorenzo laughed and called for the bill.

The maître d' smiled. "It's already been taken care of, signor," he said, nodding in the direction of Paolo, "by your old school friend."

"How kind of him," said Gian Lorenzo.

"No, her," the Contessa reminded him.

"Please excuse me for a moment," said Gian Lorenzo. "I must just thank them before we leave." He rose from his place, and made his way slowly across the crowded room.

"How are you?" said Paolo, who was on his feet long before Gian Lorenzo had reached their table. "You know my little angel, of course," he said, turning to smile at his wife, "but then how could you ever forget?"

Gian Lorenzo took Angelina's hand and kissed it gently. "And I will also never forget your magnificent wedding."

"Medici would have swooned," said Angelina.

Gian Lorenzo gave a slight bow in acknowledgment.

"Is that the Contessa di Palma you are dining with?" asked Paolo. "Because if it is, she has something my little angel desires." Gian Lorenzo made no comment. "I do hope, Gian Lorenzo, that she's a client, not a friend, because if my little angel wants something, then I will stop at nothing to ensure she gets it." Gian Lorenzo still considered it wise to remain silent. Never forget, his father had once told him, only restaurateurs close deals in restaurants—when they hand you the bill. "And as it's a field I know little about," continued Paolo, "and you are acknowledged as one of the nation's leading authorities, perhaps you would be kind enough to represent Angelina on this occasion?"

"I would be delighted to do so," said Gian Lorenzo, as the head waiter placed a chocolate trifle in front of Paolo's wife, with a bowl of crème fraîche on the side.

"Excellent," said Paolo, "let's keep in touch."

Gian Lorenzo smiled and shook his old friend by the hand. He well remembered the last occasion Paolo had made such an offer. But then some people consider such suggestions nothing more than polite conversation. Gian Lorenzo turned to Angelina and bowed low before walking back across the restaurant to rejoin the Contessa.

"Time for us to leave, I fear," said Gian Lorenzo, glancing at his watch, "especially if I'm to catch the first plane to Rome in the morning."

"Did you manage to sell my Canaletto to your friend?" asked the Contessa, as she rose from her place.

"No," replied Gian Lorenzo, as he waved in the direction of Paolo's table, "but he did suggest that we keep in touch."

"And will you?"

"That might be quite difficult," admitted Gian Lorenzo, "as he didn't give me his number, and I have a feeling Signor and Signora Castelli will not be listed in the *Yellow Pages*."

Gian Lorenzo took the first flight back to Rome the following morning. The Canaletto was to follow him at a more leisurely pace. No sooner had he set foot in the gallery than his secretary rushed out of the office, spilling out the words, "Paolo Castelli has already called twice this morning. He apologized for not giving you his number," she added, "and wondered if you would be kind enough to phone him, just as soon as you get in."

Gian Lorenzo walked calmly into his office, sat down at his desk and composed himself. He then tapped out the number his secretary had placed in front of him. The call was first answered by a butler, who transferred him to a secretary, before he was finally connected to Paolo.

"After you left last night, my little angel spoke of nothing else," began Paolo. "She has never forgotten her visit to the Contessa's home, where she first saw her magnificent art collection. She wondered if the reason you were meeting with the Contessa was—"

"I don't think it would be wise to discuss this matter over the phone," said Gian Lorenzo, whose father had also taught him that deals are rarely made on the telephone, but almost always face to face. One needs the client to view the picture, and then you allow them to hang it on a wall in their home for several days. There is a crucial moment when the buyer considers the painting already belongs to them. Not until then do you start to negotiate the price.

"Then you'll have to return to Venice," said Paolo matter-of-factly. "I'll send the private jet."

Gian Lorenzo flew to Venice the following Friday. A Rolls-Royce was parked on the runway, waiting to take him to the Villa Rosa.

A butler greeted Gian Lorenzo at the front door before escorting him up a large marble staircase to a suite of private rooms that exhibited barren walls—an art dealer's fantasy. Gian Lorenzo was reminded of the collection that his father had put together for Agnelli over a period of thirty years, now considered to be one of the finest in private hands.

Gian Lorenzo spent most of the Saturday—between meals—being escorted round the one hundred and forty-two rooms of the Villa Rosa by Angelina. He quickly discovered that there was far more to his hostess than he had anticipated.

Angelina showed a genuine interest in wanting to start her own art collection, and had clearly visited all the great galleries round the world. Gian Lorenzo concluded that she only lacked the courage of her own convictions—a not uncommon problem for the only child of a self-made man— although she didn't lack knowledge or, to Gian Lorenzo's surprise, taste. He felt guilty for making assumptions based only on comments he had read in the press. Gian Lorenzo found himself enjoying Angelina's company, and even began to wonder what this shy, thoughtful young woman could possibly see in Paolo.

Over dinner that night, Gian Lorenzo could not miss the adoration in her eyes whenever Angelina looked at her husband, even though she rarely interrupted him.

Over breakfast the following morning, Angelina hardly uttered a word. It was not until Paolo suggested that his wife show their guest round the grounds that his little angel once again came alive.

Angelina escorted Gian Lorenzo round a sixty-acre garden that possessed no immovable objects, or even havens where they might rest to cool their brows. Whenever Gian Lorenzo made a suggestion, she responded with enthusiasm, clearly willing to be led, if only he would take her by the hand.

Over dinner that night, it was Paolo who confirmed that it was his little angel's desire to build a great collection in memory of her late father.

"But where to begin?" asked Paolo, stretching a hand across the table to take his wife's hand.

"Canaletto, perhaps?" suggested Gian Lorenzo.

Gian Lorenzo spent the next five years commuting between Rome and Venice as he continued to coax pictures out of the Contessa, before rehanging them in the Villa Rosa. But as each new gem appeared, Angelina's appetite only became more voracious. Gian Lorenzo found himself having to travel as far afield as America, Russia and even Colombia, so that he could keep Paolo's "little angel" satisfied. She seemed determined to outdo Catherine the Great.

Angelina became more and more captivated by each new masterpiece Gian Lorenzo put before her—Canaletto, Caravaggio, Tintoretto, Bellini and Da Vinci were among the natives. Not only did Gian Lorenzo begin to fill up the few remaining places on the walls of the villa, but he also had statues crated and sent from every quarter of the globe to be sited alongside other immigrants on the vast lawn—Moore, Brancusi, Epstein, Miró, Giacometti and, Angelina's favorite, Botero.

With every new purchase she made, Gian Lorenzo presented her with a book about the artist. Angelina would devour them in one sitting and immediately demand more. Gian Lorenzo had to acknowledge that she had become not only the gallery's most important client but also his most ardent student—what had begun as a flirtation with Canaletto was fast turning into a promiscuous affair with almost all the great masters of Europe. And it was Gian Lorenzo who was expected to continually supply new lovers. Something else Angelina had in common with Catherine the Great.

Gian Lorenzo was visiting a client in Barcelona, who for tax reasons had to dispose of a Murillo, *The Birth of Christ*, when he heard the news. He considered that the asking price for the painting was too high, even though he knew that Angelina would be willing to pay it. He was in the middle of haggling when his secretary called. Gian Lorenzo took the next available flight back to Rome.

Every paper reported, some in great detail, the death of Angelina Castelli. A massive heart attack while she was in her garden trying to move one of the statues.

The tabloids, unwilling to mourn the lady for a single day, went on to inform their readers in the second paragraph that she had left her entire fortune to her husband. A photograph of a smiling Paolo—taken long before her death—ran alongside the story.

Four days later Gian Lorenzo flew to Venice to attend the funeral.

The little chapel in the grounds of the Villa Rosa was packed with Angelina's family and friends, some of whom Gian Lorenzo hadn't seen since the wedding celebration, a generation before.

When the six pallbearers carried the coffin into the chapel, and lowered it gently on a bier in front of the altar, Paolo broke down and sobbed. After the service was over, Gian Lorenzo offered his condolences, and Paolo assured him that he had enriched Angelina's life beyond recompense. He went on to say that he intended to continue building the collection in her memory. "It is no more than my little angel would have wanted," he explained, "so it must be done."

Paolo didn't get in touch with him again.

Gian Lorenzo was about to dip a spoon into a pot of Oxford marmalade—another habit he had acquired from his father—when he saw the headline. The spoon remained lodged in the marmalade while he read the words a second time. He wanted to be sure that he hadn't misunderstood the headline. Paolo was back on the front page, declaring it was "love at first sight—turn to page 22 for details."

Gian Lorenzo quickly flicked through the pages to a column he rarely troubled himself with. "*Gossip Roma*, we give you the truth behind the stories." Paolo Castelli, former captain of Roma, and the ninth richest man in Italy, is to marry again, only four years after the death of his little angel. "There's more to her than meets the eye," declared the headline. The paper went on to assure its readers that there couldn't be a bigger contrast between his first wife, Angelina, a billionairess, and Gina, a twenty-four-year-old waitress from Naples, and the daughter of a tax inspector.

Gian Lorenzo chuckled when he saw Gina's photograph, aware that many of Paolo's friends wouldn't be able to resist teasing him.

Every morning Gian Lorenzo found himself turning to *Gossip Roma*, in the hope of learning some new titbit about the forth-coming marriage. The wedding, it seemed, would be held in the chapel of the Villa Rosa, which only had enough space to seat a mere two hundred, so the guests would be restricted to close family and friends. The bride could no longer leave her little home without being pursued by a legion of paparazzi. The groom, they informed their readers, had returned to the gym, in the hope of losing a few pounds before the ceremony took place. But the biggest surprise for Gian Lorenzo came when *Gossip Roma* claimed—in an exclusive—that Signor Gian Lorenzo Venici, Roma's leading art dealer, and old school chum of Paolo, would be among the fortunate guests.

An invitation arrived in the morning post the following day.

Gian Lorenzo flew into Venice on the evening before the ceremony and checked into the Hotel Cipriani. He decided a light meal and an early night might perhaps be wise when he thought about the previous wedding.

Gian Lorenzo rose early the following morning and took some time dressing for the occasion. Despite this, he still arrived at the Villa Rosa long before the service was due to commence. He wished to stroll among the statues that littered the lawn and become reacquainted with some old friends. Donatello smiled down on him. Moore looked regal. Miró made him laugh, and Giacometti stood tall and thin, but his favorite remained the fountain which graced the center of the lawn. Ten years before he had removed each piece of the fountain, stone by stone, statue by statue, from a courtyard in Milan. Bellini's *The Escaping Hunter* looked even more magnificent in its new surroundings. It gave Gian Lorenzo particular pleasure to see how many other guests had also arrived early, clearly with the same thought in mind.

A single usher in a smart dark suit walked among the guests suggesting that they might like to make their way to the chapel as the ceremony was about to begin. Gian Lorenzo was one of the first to heed his advice, as he wanted to be well placed to watch the bride make her entrance.

Gian Lorenzo found a vacant seat on the aisle about halfway back that would allow him an uninterrupted view of the proceedings. He could see the little choir in their stalls, already singing vespers accompanied by a string quartet.

At five minutes to three Paolo and his best man entered the chapel and walked slowly down the aisle. Gian Lorenzo knew he'd been a well-known footballer, but he still couldn't remember his name. They both took their places by the side of the altar, while Paolo waited for his young bride to appear. Paolo looked fit, tanned and trim, and Gian Lorenzo noted that women still stared at him with adoring eyes. Paolo didn't notice them and a grin that would have excited comment from Lewis Carroll never left the bridegroom's face.

There was a buzz of expectation as the string quartet struck up the opening chords of the Wedding March, to herald the entrance of the bride. The young woman walked slowly down the aisle on the arm of her father, and drew intakes of breath as she passed each new row.

Gian Lorenzo could hear her approaching, so he turned to look at Gina for the first time. How would he respond, when asked to describe the bride, to someone who hadn't been invited to the ceremony? Should he emphasize her beautiful long, thick, raven hair, or possibly comment on the smooth olive texture of her skin, or even add some remark about the magnificent wedding dress that he remembered so well? Or would Gian Lorenzo simply tell all those who inquired that it had become immediately clear to him why Paolo had declared that it was love at first sight. The same shy smile as Angelina, the same bright enthusiastic twinkle in her eyes, the same gentleness that was clear for all to see, or was it, as Gian Lorenzo suspected, that the journalists would only report that she fitted snugly into Angelina's old wedding dress—the yards and yards of silk forming a magnificent train behind the bride as she walked slowly toward her lover.

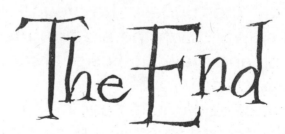

The End